PAYBACK IS A WITCH

MAYA DANIELS

By Maya Daniels

Chronicles of Forbidden Witchery

Resting Witch Face
Pitch a Witch
Witch Please
Payback is a Witch

Vinci Books

vinci-books.com

Published by Vinci Books Ltd in 2025

1

Copyright © Maya Daniels 2024

The author has asserted their moral right to be identified as the author of this work in accordance with the Copyright, Designs and Patents Act 1988. This work is a work of fiction. Names, characters, places and incidents are the product of the author's imagination or are used fictitiously. Any resemblance to actual persons, living or dead, places and incidents is entirely coincidental.

All rights reserved. No part of this publication may be copied, reproduced, distributed, stored in any retrieval system, or transmitted in any form or by any means, including photocopying, recording, or other electronic or mechanical methods, nor used as a source for any form of machine learning including AI datasets, without the prior written permission of the publisher.

The publisher and the author have made every effort to obtain permissions for any third party material used in this book and to comply with copyright law. Any queries in this respect should be brought to the attention of the publisher and any omissions will be corrected in future editions.

A CIP catalogue record for this book is available from the British Library.

Paperback ISBN: 9781036705817

Chapter One

Lesson 16: *If you can't beat them, join them, although old habits die hard.*

I didn't follow anyone, by principle.

I learned this one on the day as I stood at the bottom of the steps leading toward the great double doors of my coven building, more so than any other time of my life. I couldn't say why to save my life, and it truly pissed me off.

My eyes traveled slowly from the bottom of the steps, over the monstrosity of the building, until they settled on the very top of the glass dome, and I swallowed thickly the fear that tried to claw its way up my throat. While I was too busy self-loathing and doing my best not to die, they rebuilt the damage I caused to the structure, not once but twice.

Just as I was rounding the corner at the edge of the last bookshelf, my shoulder bumped into a line of stacked books protruding from it. It made me stagger, and the grimoire I had in my hands dropped on the floor with a heavy thud. That was followed by another smack when the damn book, which jabbed me in the arm, hit the ground too, falling on the spine, and it flopped open somewhere in the middle. An invisible breeze skirted across my skin, and goosebumps covered my arms. My heart jammed in my windpipe, and I flipped around, searching for some asshole with air magic trying to pull a prank on me.

But no one was in the library other than me.

Dread pooled in my stomach, and I really didn't want to be in the damn room anymore. The first traces of dawn were peeking through the tall windows, casting purples and pinks over the wooden shelves and leather tomes. What little light was poking through the brightening sky pierced the liquid in the jars, giving all the eyeballs, fingers, and such a menacing vibe. I had every intention of snatching the grimoire and hightailing it out of there, but when I bent at the waist to grab it, the text on the opened book got my attention. It was a siren song overtaking my mind.

I was powerless to resist it.

A horn blared somewhere in the distance, dragging me out of whatever rabbit hole my damaged brain cells were pulling me into, and I realized my fists were balled so tightly that my nails were cutting through the skin of my wet palms.

"You are seriously pathetic," I muttered to myself as I wiped my sweaty palms off my pants in disgust. "Witches don't get PTSD. Get your shit together, girl."

The pentagram on the side of my finger tingled at that, reminding me that my life was no longer the same. I was no longer that same person every member of the coven gossiped about and whispered insults behind her back. Well, they still did that, but for entirely different reasons now.

I was no longer a dud.

I was the monster all of them feared.

Even Danika thought twice before squaring off with me these days.

Yet again. Here I was….

A scared little mouse with shaky knees, too afraid to kick in the damn doors and walk in like I owned the place.

I was seriously pathetic and should be put down immediately—preferably in my designer clothing. I would turn in my grave if I ended up in the afterlife dressed in polyester.

A shiver skirted up my spine.

Instead of keeling over right then and there, with each step I counted the slow exhales of my breaths until I was certain that my heartbeats no longer resembled a galloping racehorse while making sure that no one saw the ridiculous display of weakness. Stupid, I knew, but as I said, old habits died hard. Deep down I was still the old Hazel. The one that hid her inadequacy behind a smart mouth, lots of bravado and a legendary sense of fashion if I could say so myself. My designer shoes and the leather wrapped around me could attest to that last statement even to a blind person.

On one side though, a very hidden -don't even tell myself where it was- space, I liked the new Hazel better. She was everything I ever wanted to be while growing up thinking I had zero gifts. Powerful supernaturals cowered in front of the force of her magic. It was who I prayed to the Goddess to make me when I was growing up. What I never expected was for the people I cared about to be near constant threat of dying because of it. I wanted magic so bad so I could protect them better, not get them killed faster. For that reason, that part of the new me I disliked with a passion as much as I loved it.

Which was the main reason I now stood in front of the closed doors of my coven, staring up at the three red keys marking it as a tribute to Hecate. None of the skeleton keys were crooked, and they all looked brand new—as if the Goddess herself was pointing out to me that no matter how powerful I was, she could erase me from existence without a second thought. Like I never existed. Deep down, I was sure that I was working on borrowed time and had to do something before it was too late.

Something had to change, and I knew just the person to talk to about it. The problem I had was I had to swallow my pride along with the newly formed lump in my throat, to actually walk in and get it over with.

Danika didn't bite. I mean, what could she do now? She couldn't kill me if she tried.

I should've asked Sissily to come with me, but I thought she could use a day off from my drama. Good thing too because she never would've let me forget it when the double doors unexpectedly opened and I jumped almost a foot in the air. Luckily, I clamped my mouth shut and only a tiny squeak escaped me, hopefully low enough that the person barging through the damn entrance didn't hear it.

The male that walked out was someone I'd seen in passing a lot around the coven, but I couldn't remember his name to save my life.

"Hecate help me, Miss Byrne." The middle-aged witch gasped, pressing a flat palm at the center of his chest. "You scared me."

My glare reminded him that on the best of days I was not a friendly person for that type of a conversation, so he rushed to backtrack in the same breath. "I just didn't expect anyone to be standing there, that's all. Not that *you* are scary." My glower deepened more at that, and he gulped, going as far as taking a step back and bumping the slowly closing door which made him jump a little to the side instead, as if physical difference would save him from my anger.

My magic reared its ugly head with those thoughts, churning at the center of my chest like a cobra waiting to strike. What was worse, was the fact that I felt justified in attacking him according to the emotions filling my head. And all that from a simple, accidental bump in passing.

Who was I? What in the goddess's name was happening to me?

I despised bullies. I was *not* a bully.

Fear from the monster I was becoming overshadowed anything my powers could artificially produce inside my head, so I shook off the daze which was forcing its way to the surface. As much as I loved Danika, despite all the skeletons coming out of the closet and everything she'd done, I never wanted to become like her in that sense. I was an asshole, not an evil bitch. Still, I had a reputation to uphold that would hopefully keep people away from me. I never wanted to be a monster, but approachable I certainly was not.

"I could try harder if I'm not scary enough like this." Dust could've puffed out of my lips from the dryness of my tone as I cocked a hip and slapped my hand on it.

"I simply meant I didn't expect anyone to be anywhere near the coven at this hour, Miss Byrne." The male attempted to mold himself to one side of the door and mumbled almost to himself while color was draining from his face with each word. "It is the middle of the day."

"You are here," I told him reasonably; you'd think we were discussing the weather.

"I suppose you are correct." With a nervous chuckle that sounded more like a wheeze he slumped on the partially opened door, and I watched with rapt interest how a drop of sweat rolled down one side of his face.

"Doing what exactly?" My eyes narrowed and zoomed in like a hawk on the male for a totally different reason now.

"I beg your pardon?"

"You are here in the middle of the day when no one is around, doing what exactly that makes you so jumpy?" Speaking slowly and deliberately, I folded my arms across my chest and waited. When he said nothing for at least five seconds, my shoe started tapping and broke through the tense silence.

I'd learned that one from Sissily. It was proven to be an unnerving tactic when someone was trying to hide something. At least with me it was. Almost like a hot poker to my brain with each tap every time my friend did it.

"But...but...but..." the male stuttered, rearing his head up, straightening and unfolding like a constipated flamingo. Blush started spreading up, pinkening his neck within seconds from his anger at my interrogation.

See how much I cared about his outrage.

"But, but, but... What, sir?" Stabbing a French manicured finger at his rapidly reddening face, I squinted at him. "It's a simple question. Answer it!"

"If you are accusing me of some nefarious reasons for being inside this building, Miss Byrne, I will have no other choice but to bring this up with your grandmother." Squaring his shoulders, the so far meek-appearing male stuck his nose up so he could look down it at me. "I am a respected member of this coven and will not allow myself to be questioned like a common crook. Not even by you." Yanking on his collared shirt unnecessarily, he puffed out his chest.

"That still didn't answer my question," I deadpanned, as the right side of my mouth twisted in annoyance. Would it be such a terrible thing if I socked him in the head, I thought to myself?

Another horn blaring, this one much closer than the one before, destroyed the built-up tension I had created hoping to make the male talk. Not that I had a feeling he was doing something wrong. But I'd learned the hard way that these days I couldn't trust anyone or anything. Check first, trust later.

Look at me all grown up.

I was ready to pat myself on the back when the male hunched down and gave me all of two seconds before he tackled me out of nowhere. All the air was pushed out of my chest with a loud grunt when my back hit the pavement hard enough I heard one of my ribs crack. The back of my skull followed with a resounding smack on the patterned marble and black roses bloomed in front of my eyes while nausea churned in my gut.

"Motherfuc..." I wheezed a second before a fist was jabbed in my side, forcing me to involuntarily curl up so I could protect my organs. The asshole was doing his damn best to relocate my kidneys, I would've asked if he was a nephrologist if I had any breath left in me.

A few more knees and knuckles connected with parts of my body before I realized the male had no intention of stopping his assault. This was not a simple reaction to me insulting him by asking what he was doing in the building in the middle of the day as he claimed. Oh, no. As was my luck lately, I'd stumbled on some clusterfuck I would've rather avoided. Unfortunately, the douche didn't give me the option to refuse.

Sharp pain was spreading from my left shoulder all the way down to my pinky toe which was made worse when I twisted to that side in hopes to avoid another punch to my ribs. As a reward I received a fist in my left boob and saw stars spinning when my eyes rolled to the back of my head.

A scream was ripped out of me at that, but it sounded more like a yell of outrage than one caused by pain. My legs managed to wrap around his, and I hooked the heels of my shoes as best I could so he couldn't shake me off. With a sharp twist of my hips, I successfully turned us around so that he was now under me and I was straddling his thighs. The owlish look he gave me when I grinned at him through crazy strands of my messed-up hair made every punch and kick I received worth it.

"You didn't think I'd let you have all the fun the whole time, did you?" I told him when he started buckling in an attempt to get away. Laughing, I rammed my fist in his cheekbone, widening my smile when I felt it crunch under my knuckles. "How boring, darling. I prefer to be the one on top."

Holding him firmly on the ground, I returned the favor by rearranging his organs until he stopped buckling and trying to escape. When he stopped moving, so did I, and I sat fully on the back of my legs, breathing loud enough to be heard all the way to New York. My knuckles were shredded and I could feel the blood that sprayed me in the face trickle down my chin. I tried to wipe it with my forearm then grimaced when it smudged all over the sleeve of my shirt. There was no way blood was coming off the angora sweater I was wearing. I'd managed to ruin yet another shirt in the cursed coven.

"Hazel?" Ace's voice coming from the steps made me close my eyes and beg the universe for patience. "What in the world are you doing?" The soles of his combat boots thumped a soothing rhythm as he ran toward me.

"If I told you it wasn't my fault and he started it, would you believe me?" I asked with my eyes still closed.

"A fight not your fault?" The snort coming out of him as his shadow fell over me, darkening the midday sun, spoke volumes. "No."

"I didn't think so." On a heavy sigh, I pushed myself up and stood to face him.

"You're bleeding," Ace snarled, all humor leaving his features as he stepped too close for my comfort and reached for my face.

"Yeah, well." Jerking away from his fingers I sidestepped to put distance between us in case he made a grab for me. "You should've seen the other guy." He looked unimpressed at my joke, his wolf flashing briefly in his irises, but I had other things to worry about instead of Ace's feelings. "You gonna help me carry him inside or you don't want to dirty your clothes? I need to know what he was doing here that made it worth it to attack me when I caught him leaving."

Not Ace but a predator watched me contemplatively for a long moment through narrowed eyes. Stubbornly, I kept my gaze locked on the shifter as best I could since one of my eyes was slowly swelling up. Without a word, he bent over and snatched the passed-out male from the ground, unceremoniously tossing him over his shoulder. Stunned, I watched his back retreating for a long second before I snapped out of it and rushed to catch up with him.

"Such a gentleman." I wheezed, holding my side and hating my pretty shoes at that moment. I could bet my newfound magic that my compliment did not impress the wolf.

Chapter Two

"No!" Both my arms stretched toward Ace as he was about to drop the unconscious male on the floor in Danika's empty office. You'd think I could physically stop him if he was dead set on dropping his cargo. "Put him on the couch, not on the floor." When the shifter turned to look at me with a cocked eyebrow, I smirked. "That stupid furniture is a lot more uncomfortable than the thick oriental rugs that cost a year's worth of a witch's salary. Believe me."

"Most of the time I don't understand you, Hazel." He still walked up to the stupid piece of furniture and dropped the male like a rock on it. "I see what you mean," he added, his lips twisting in distaste after hearing the smack of the guy's head on the couch as if it had hit a stone and not a cushioned seat.

"She doesn't want anyone feeling comfortable in her presence." I told him in passing as I beelined for the liquor cabinet on the other side of the office. "It's part of her charm."

Snatching a rocks glass, I passed my pointer finger over

the lined-up bottles until I found a bottle of Macallan anniversary malt. A fifty-year-old whisky that would give Danika an aneurism when she saw it opened and hopefully —by the time she came to the office—half empty, as well. From the corner of my eye, I watched Ace cringe when I slugged the first glass like a tequila shot and followed it with two more before I turned and pointed the bottle at him.

"You want some?"

The tip of my tongue kept poking at my split lip which was burning from the alcohol that managed to escape the rim of the glass. Ace homed in on it like a hawk, his nostrils flaring, but the second my eyes narrowed at him, he visibly took a deep breath and shook off whatever ideas started circling in his head.

"I was asking you about the whisky."

"I know what you were asking." With a shake of his head, he turned around and walked all the way to the massive desk before he faced me again. "How about telling me why you're here and not behind pack walls where it's safe."

"Alex knows I left." There was no escaping the defensiveness in my tone. I hated that his lips twitched and he fought a smile. I was not a youngling, damn it. I could go wherever I wanted without asking permission.

"He told me." The shifter even lifted a hand, palm facing me, to stop whatever else was going to spill from my mouth. "That's why I came. To make sure you're okay."

"I'm okay," I blurted before he was done talking and then gulped the remaining whisky from the glass.

"I can see that you're just fine." Disappointment colored his voice. "Hopefully, you'll be able to see through both eyes in a week. The lip will heal in a day or two. So that's great news."

"Your snide comments are not needed, Ace." Turning my back on him, I poured another glass. "Maybe, if you're bored instead of following me around you can find a hobby or something. I hear crochet is the vibe nowadays. You should give it a whirl. I'm a big girl. I'll take care of myself."

He just silently stared at me for long enough that I felt a need to start fidgeting. I could feel his gaze between my shoulder blades like the end of a barrel from a loaded gun. Goosebumps puckered the skin of my arms. On a huff, I turned to face him and almost fell to the side when the alcohol hit my brain. Catching myself on the open door of the cabinet, I dared him to say anything about it. Like the wise male that he was, he kept his lips sealed.

"I came to talk to Danika." Whether it was the whisky or the blood-loss, I had no clue, but all the fight left me in a blink of an eye, and I just felt sore and tired. "Now that I have somewhat control of my magic, I would be more useful here than tucked away in a room while the rest of you are fighting my battles."

Ace stayed quiet, leaning back on the desk and watching me expectantly. Before I could make a fool of myself and fall down where I was standing I pressed back on the liquor cabinet and slid down until my butt kissed the expensive rugs my grandmother liked. Lifting the bottle closer to my face, I squinted at it, admiring the strength of the drink. I had to remember that this one did the trick if I wanted to get drunk fast. It went down smooth and nice but packed a punch like an elephant.

"This is some good stuff," I told the bottle.

"I bet." Ace snorted and snatched it from my fingers before I could realize that he had moved and was looming over me. "And you've had enough of it for now."

"Hey." My attempt at getting it back made him laugh

out loud at me as he danced effortlessly out of my reach. "Give that back."

Instead of doing what I asked, he took my drink away and returned with a glass of water from the water dispenser tucked behind my grandmother's desk. I glared at him when he brought it over but took it anyway and drained it without stopping for breath. Someone must've seen the fight in front of the coven or us carrying the male in her office over Ace's shoulder and snitched to Danika. I had no doubt that she was already on her way, and I wanted to be able to stand when she arrived.

Ace brought me two more full to the brim glasses of water which I gulped down without protest. When he turned to get more, I grabbed his pant leg to stop him, shaking my head instead of using words to communicate. It took me a good half hour to stop feeling dizzy and breathe properly without fear of expelling the expensive whisky from my body.

"What do you think he was doing here in the middle of the day?" Rubbing at my temples, I leaned the back of my head on the cabinet behind me. "I didn't think there were that many brave souls to try and go behind Danika's back. She's going to be pissed."

"For all we know he could've been having an affair and meeting in the coven during the day with his lover." Ace shrugged a shoulder but frowned at the still unconscious male before focusing back on me. "You did a number on him. It might be a while before we can ask him."

"Was I supposed to let him beat me to death?" I asked incredulously.

"I'm actually more impressed that you used your fists and not your magic." Stepping closer to the couch, he lifted his foot and nudged the male in the thigh. When the witch didn't immediately wake up, he kicked him harder with the same result. "We would've needed a dust pan if you'd zapped him with it." Looking over his shoulder at my open mouth, he chuckled. "What? I've seen what happens when someone pisses you off."

"I have better control over it now," was all I said instead of taking the bait and starting an argument. "Maybe we should've checked to see if there was anyone else in the building. Although no one was at the assistant desk in front of Danika's office either. If that's any indication, the building is empty and only protected with the wards."

Ace just stared at me as if he didn't believe me when I claimed that I had better control of my magic and that truly made me want to snap at him, but the whisky was still churning in my stomach, so I refrained from anything that required me to get animated and stand up. I needed my butt cheeks firmly planted on the rug, thank you very much.

"It's daytime outside." Waiting to see if my words hit the mark, I almost laughed when the shifter narrowed his gaze. "The humans are already afraid of us as is. The last thing we need is for me to start throwing magic around in mid-day and turn people into anthills. I can live with a split lip and a swollen eye. I can't live with the fact I made them fear us enough that they turn on us." I started to reach for my face so I could scrub a hand over it but luckily caught myself in time before I pressed on all the injuries which were already slowly healing. "They won't stop with the witches, either. I won't be the reason we all go down."

"Nobody is going down." Danika's voice made my hunched spine snap straight and I scrambled to stand up before she fully stepped into her office.

"Eavesdropping is rude," I muttered under my breath but my heart skipped a beat when her head snapped to the side and she nailed me with those cold green eyes. "I'm just saying." Dumbly, I continued talking, so I pressed my lips tight and bit on them from the inside of my mouth to keep them from parting.

"Ace. What brings you here?" Danika dismissed me as per usual and sashayed behind her desk where she lowered in the leather chair as gracefully as a swan. "I was not expecting visitors today."

"He's with me." I jumped to his rescue before she could cause problems for him with his Alpha. "I wanted to come talk to you and he came to make sure I'm okay."

Danika leaned forward, pressing her forearms on the desk and looked me up and down with a speculative gaze which tied a knot in my gut. I was a mess, covered in blood with bloody knuckles, stained shirt and a swollen eye. My appearance called me a liar so my grandmother didn't have to.

"Ace was parking the car when this dude"—I stabbed a finger at the male starfishing it on her couch while I continued my explanation—"attacked me at the doors."

"Why in Hecate's name would Mr. Seaward be attacking you?" Taken by surprise, she released me from her glare and looked at the guy I was pointing at. I realized that she didn't notice him until that moment. With a groan, she closed her eyes and pressed the bridge of her nose between a thumb and a forefinger. "What did you do now, Hazel?"

"Why doesn't anyone believe me when I say I was attacked and didn't initiate a fight?" Glancing from Ace to Danika, who didn't look impressed at all, I threw both my arms in the air. "Did you miss the part where I said he attacked me? I asked him what he was doing in the building in the middle of the day and he turned feral. He tackled me."

"We brought him here so we could question him when you arrived." Ace, ever the helpful, chirped in to back me up as lame as his attempts appeared to be.

My grandmother rose from the chair like a cobra uncoiling just before a strike and I had never been so happy that her cold, murderous glare was not aimed at me. She rounded the desk with such fluidity it seemed like she was gliding over the rugs instead of walking, her long black dress curling gently around her feet. I held my breath when she came close until she stopped at the head of the unconscious form.

"We shall know now what he was doing." Snatching the guy's arm so fast I barely saw her move, she yanked him off the couch with such ease that my jaw hit the floor. "Wake up, Seaward." She shook him as if he weighed nothing.

When nothing happened, I cleared my throat which earned me a glower for interrupting. "I might've hurt him more than I intended."

Ace choked on a laugh at my offhanded comment, but he covered it with a cough. It still didn't fool my grandmother who sent him a side-eyed look which promised painful things for the shifter if he did it again.

Another shock smacked me on the side of the head when she reached behind her and, simply by curling her fingers, dragged a heavy chair next to her. Plonking the male on it, she grabbed his chin and squeezed hard, jerking his face up. "I said wake up, Seaward." Her red painted nails sunk into the skin of his cheeks like claws.

Power burst out of Danika the moment she drew blood. Like a blast of a bomb, it exploded out of her and filled the room with magic so potent all the short hairs of my body were standing on end. Poor Ace latched onto the back of the now empty couch, fighting a shift with everything in him. The air smelled like ozone, and it stung my nostrils.

"Wha..." the witch mumbled, blinking his eyes fast in poor attempts to focus on my grandmother's face.

Groaning, the male tried to curl up in a ball, hugging his middle, but Danika held firmly to his face. So he kept wiggling feebly until he finally had his eyelids peeled back and could see his predicament.

"Mrs. Byrne." The male gasped. "I... Where... how..."

"Speak." Danika said it so calmly that fear lodged in my throat like a fist.

The dude pissed himself.

I couldn't blame him.

Until he started searching around for help with his eyes and he spotted me to the side. "She attacked me unprovoked." I didn't need to be a shifter or a vamp to know the high-pitched squeal stunk of lies. "She hurt me."

"Dude, don't lie. Just tell her the truth before you regret delaying it." I was surprised when I found that I genuinely wanted him to tell her so she didn't hurt him. Not that it would back up my story. Although, that didn't hurt.

"She hurt me," the witch repeated, but doubt was loud and clear in the tentative tone of his voice.

"You have never seen pain like I would inflict if you do not speak." Danika bent at the waist until they were nose to nose.

It was all of two seconds before he started screaming, and I wanted to be anywhere but in that room.

Chapter Three

"You okay, kiddo?" Alex's mismatched eyes found me nearly twelve hours later before he'd even fully entered the almost empty office that used to belong to High priest Shadowblood, may the goddess torment his soul for all eternity.

"Ace the snitch called you, huh?" My mouth twisted in a grimace as I contemplated how to repay the treacherous shifter for the betrayal.

Since the alpha just stood there staring at me intently as if he had x-ray vision and could confirm for himself that I was as well as when I left his house, I waved at the space next to me on the bare floor so he could join me instead of looming over my head ominously.

"I knew I should've come with you." With a huff, he grumbled under his nose and shook his head, stomping across the space so he could plop next to me.

"He shouldn't have called you." Raising my hand to stop his argument, I leaned the back of my head on the wall and closed my eyes. "You have a pack to run and family to take care of. I'm a big girl. Believe it or not I could take care of myself."

"If I didn't believe that, I wouldn't have let you out of my sight." Nudging my shoulder with his, he forced me to turn my head and look at him. "After facing off with Leviathan and coming out not just alive but well enough to give Danika attitude, I believe you can take care of all of us, not just yourself." His thick forefinger popped between us when I opened my mouth to say something. "It doesn't mean I'll stop worrying about you, kid. With all we've been through, you are like one of my own runts now."

"I'll tell Amber that you're calling her precious children runts." At the horrified expression on his face, I had to bark out a laugh so unexpectedly I choked on my own spit. All the humor left me however as he started pounding on my back in an attempt to help me. Sharp pains spread through my upper body with such intensity I cried out before I could stop myself.

"Hazel?" Alex lifted both his hands in surrender, jerking away from me as if I'd burned him. "I didn't hit that hard. What's wrong?"

"Wait." I wheezed, holding a hand between us to stop him from trying to smack my back or talk, I had no idea which. It was unnecessary to say the least because the mountain of a male shrunk back away from me as far as he could without getting up. "I'm okay...I'm okay."

"I would disagree, kid." The wary way he was eying me told me he expected me to break down into sobs or literally fall apart so that he would have to reattach my limbs. "What in the worlds happened here?"

I opened my mouth again to say that I was fine, but his eyebrows shot up all the way to his hairline and murder burst into life in his mismatched eyes, effectively shutting me up with a snap. "Does all that screaming have something to do with why you're in pain? May the universe help me, Hazel, but Danika will answer to me if she has hurt you."

He was already halfway up to march down and shake Danika from her expensive shoes, but I snatched the edge of his t-shirt and yanked him down. We were both surprised that I managed to pull him to the floor.

"I stumbled onto something when I came to the coven. The male didn't like that I interrupted his business, so he attacked me. I didn't expect him to do that." A snort escaped me at the dumb way I handled the situation. "He got a few good hits before I upper-handed him." At the doubtful look Alex gave me, I twisted my mouth in distaste. "Okay, fine. He did a number on me before my brain to fists connection was restored. You should've seen him, Alex. He looks like he can't pick up anything heavier than a cup of tea."

"Since when do you underestimate anyone based on their appearance?" The lecturing tone of his voice hurt more than any fists ever could.

"I was today years old when I learned that I can be dumb on occasion." With a self-deprecating shrug, I petted his raised knee. "I should've known better than to have my guard down, but I was too worked up about asking Danika to let me back in that I was oblivious to everything else. I'm pathetic."

"I heard my name." The door suddenly opened, and my grandmother floated inside on silent feet effectively cutting off anything Alex was about to say.

My heart tried to jump out through my mouth and escape but I swallowed it down with great effort. "Of course, you did." I hated that she had that effect on me. I was not a child anymore, damn it. "Even the walls have ears in this place, yet no one had a clue that something fishy was going on."

"Do not presume to lecture me on how to run my coven, Hazel Byrne. Magic or not, you are still under my authority." The icebergs in the North Pole had more warmth than the expression on Danika's face or her tone.

I'd liked to pretend that she was just angry because of the male I caught doing whatever he was doing behind her back, but I knew better. That fury which turned the green of her eyes as cold and as sharp as glass was reserved only for me. I'd seen it enough times to have no doubt about it. Resentment bubbled hot and fast at the center of my chest, and my mouth opened although I knew I should bite my tongue.

"I do not presume anything, Grandmother." My sneer took not just her by surprise but me as well.

"Do we know what the male was trying to hide?" Alex spoke so calmly and nonchalantly like we were not about to start throwing magic at each other.

Both Danika and I turned to gape at him with our lips slightly parted. Me, with a stupefied expression on my face was a common sight. Danika was a totally different matter and I watched Alex incredulously as he fought a smile. The Alpha had balls of steel, I'd say that much.

"No." My grandmother narrowed her predatory gaze on the Alpha, and I didn't like the calculative look she gave him. "*We*, don't know. Yet." The way she dragged the 'we,' suggested he was not part of whatever equated as we in the situation.

Protective instincts rose in me to stand between the Alpha and whatever threat he was facing, so I followed the urge without thinking twice. Standing up, I placed myself between them, jutting my chin up at my grandmother's glare. There was no reason to second guess my instincts. Danika may be my blood but actions proved that Alex was family. If she wanted to get to him, she would have to go through me first. I made that abundantly clear to her and had no regrets for my action.

"We"—sticking a thumb over my shoulder at Alex who was still silently sitting on the floor, I turned it at myself next, pressing the tip of my nail to my chest—"would like to be kept in the loop. If *you* don't mind. After all the bruises and aches I received to hold that bastard down, I deserve that much."

"You could've used magic," Danika mocked me, a smirk tugging on one corner of her mouth that lacked humor.

Ever since I'd told her about our not so nice meet and greet with Leviathan in his realm and all the pearls he'd let slip, Danika had been acting strange. Making little jabs every chance she got about my newly found magic and how undeserving or inadequate I was to have such power. In other words, she couldn't deal well with having another person as powerful as she was around. Not that I was fully ready to use whatever gifts I had. But I wasn't as pathetic as when I'd blown up the building that first time, either.

"I could've killed him, too, instead of giving you the opportunity to interrogate him, but here we are." And just because I had a death wish and never learned to keep my trap shut, I grinned widely at her. "Besides, someone once told me that with great power comes even greater responsibility." Alex choked a laugh behind me but covered it with a cough. "Which is why I resorted to physical altercation in the middle of the day where humans were gawking at us. I know how much appearances matter to you, Grandmother. I wouldn't dare sully your reputation."

Danika watched me with single-minded focus for long

enough that an itch developed on the nostril on the left side of my face, and I was dying to scratch it but didn't dare break eye contact. What I lacked in experience when it came to winning battles with magic I made up for with stubbornness—especially in staring, or glaring as the case was at that moment. The whisky I'd gulped down had started to churn in my stomach as well as intensifying the acid that slowly crept up my throat. Still, I started at Danika unblinking, not backing down to save my life.

"Why are you here, Hazel?" After an uncomfortably long time, she expelled a long sigh and released me from her gaze.

"What? I need permission to come to my coven now?" I meant it to sound snarky, but it came out defensive and hurt.

When Alex placed a plate sized hand on my shoulder and squeezed to tell me that he was there and had my back always, tears pricked at the back of my eyes, but I blinked them away. Blowing out a breath, I shook my head to physically disperse all the argumentative thoughts that were fighting to come out. Danika didn't miss the gesture from the Alpha, and she was not very pleased, judging by the muscle that started ticking on one side of her jaw.

"Sorry." I swallowed my pride and locked gazes with Danika without any bravado this time. "That was uncalled for, but I'm still riled up from the fight and everything else. I hope you won't hold it against me."

The lift of one perfectly shaped eyebrow was my only answer.

"I came to ask you to put me back on the roster for city patrol."

"You were never on the roster," she drawled, but I acted like I didn't hear her. That was semantics.

Taking a fast breath before she would dismiss me, I rushed to convince her. "I have control of my magic now. Alex can confirm it, too. Plus, I'll be more productive here than hidden on pack lands. It's not like trouble doesn't find me there as you have witnessed yourself. At least here you'll always have an eye on me and my whereabouts." As I gave her a sharp nod for no reason, I remembered one more thing, so I stabbed a finger in the air for emphasis. "And I'll have a partner. So, I can't be wayward without you being alerted about it."

Danika squinted at me like I had some hidden agenda or something. In all honesty, I was going insane and had to be productive or I would go find someone to kill me myself.

"It's a win-win. Really." Nodding encouragingly like a bobblehead when she stayed silent, I held my breath.

"I'm willing to add one of my males to every pair you send out if you allow Hazel to join in patrols." Alex's deep voice warmed me inside like nothing ever could. "The pack still stands to protect her, no matter where she goes."

The support from the Alpha and his family ever since that cursed day I unlocked my magic had been something I never dreamed of having. I owed it to them as well as a handful of others that stood by me to do something with this power instead of hiding like a scared little girl.

"I do not believe this to be the right time for you to join our ranks, Hazel." Pinching the bridge of her nose, Danika closed her eyes briefly, allowing us for the first time to see how exhausted she was. "Mr. Greywood, as admirable as your dedication is to keeping my granddaughter safe, I am trying to keep her out of sight for a good reason. There are seven delegations arriving in Cleveland as we speak to reassess the Gatekeeper's coven and our dealings here after word has gotten out about Hazel's magic. Which I denied, of course."

I had no idea how I missed that Danika was not her perfect self. As she allowed the mask to slip, I could notice the tightness around the corners of her mouth and eyes and the rigid way she held herself. So much different from her usual effortless elegance.

"What do they want with Hazel?" The Alpha's question snapped me out of my close examination of Danika.

"They want to make sure she is not a danger to society." Her pointed look annoyed me to no end. "I need to meet with all of them first before I know how to proceed."

"You think the male sneaking around the building in the middle of the day had something to do with it?" Alex stepped away from me and started pacing a tight line next to us. A deep line formed between his eyebrows and he glared at the bare floor like it owed him a life debt. "Maybe I should try questioning him."

"Be my guest." Danika swirled a long-fingered hand in no specific direction. "He will eventually talk. I do try not to kill him, so it takes a bit longer."

Alex opened his mouth to reply, but the opening of the door had all three of us turn in that direction. Sissily popped her head in and quickly read the tension in the room as her gaze darted from Danika, to me, to Alex. Not bothering to ask whether it was okay to join us, she darted inside, slamming the door behind her and rushing to stand next to me.

"They are here," my best friend told Danika before looking me up and down. "What did I miss?"

Chapter Four

"I'm pretty sure we can sneak out when they all enter the main ritual chamber," Sissily whispered before sticking her head out of the door to see if the hallway was still empty.

Which it was. In the last nerve-wracking hour, not a soul had moved that we could see yet the crazy female insisted on checking every twenty seconds. After she announced that the delegations had arrived, Sissily got stuck with me in the empty office. Danika invited Alex to accompany her, and after firmly ordering me—and by default, Sissily as well—to stay put and not move a toe outside the room, she left us to be prisoners in a cage with a door wide open.

"I'm not running away," I told my bestie for the umpteenth time, leaning a shoulder on the wall next to where she was peeking out the door. "You can leave the door open, you know. They're looking for me and I'm hidden from view. If they see you standing there, just smile and pretend you're doing Pilates using the doorframe."

"Do I look like a crazy person to you?" Pulling back and

away from her stakeout, she turned to face me fully before blowing away a strand of hair that escaped her ponytail.

"Yes," I deadpanned, and it took everything in me not to laugh when her mouth dropped open. "Next question."

"You are such a jerk." With a huff of pretend annoyance, she thumped her forehead on the closed door. "I want to know what they're talking about."

"How much you wanna bet they are sharing recipes on how to preserve a penis in a jar?"

Sissily's laughter helped calm my nerves down if only for a moment. We snickered like high school girls remembering the time we had to clean up the library and I found a book with all sorts of crazy things in it. My best friend even had tears trickling from the corners of her eyes from laughing so hard.

"Dear goddess, my stomach hurts." Pressing a hand to her chest, she took a deep breath to stop herself from laughing. "It could be for Minotaur testicles, too, you know?" reminding me of the time I offered River Blackman the said testicles just to get him away from me.

That doubled both of us over for a good few minutes. It felt like the good old times when no one was gunning for my head and we could do whatever we wanted. As short-lived as it was, it did feel great to joke around for a moment. Seeing Sissily wipe tears of joy made it worth it.

Until something clattered in the hallway loud enough for both of us to freeze and then fall immediately quiet. Sissily watched me wide-eyed, a hand pressed to her mouth, but I raised a finger in wordless plea for silence, tilting my head and straining my ears in hopes to hear if someone was headed our way.

The freshly rebuilt office was still empty so no one should be using it for anything unless they were specifically looking for us. Or they heard us chortling like fools. I wanted to slap myself but it was too late to turn back time. Instead, using my hands and fingers, I asked Sissily to open the door and check. She swirled a finger around her temple to tell me I was nuts. As if I didn't know that already.

"Open and check," I mouthed while she stared at me, trying to lipread. Pressing my back to the wall and shaking my hands off like some boxer, I nodded encouragingly at her and raised two thumbs up.

She glared at me.

"Open." I mouthed more firmly, adding a frown for good measure, and she rolled her eyes at me.

Squaring her shoulders and petting her hair to smooth it out, my best friend took hold of the doorknob firmly enough to turn her knuckles white. Without delay, she yanked the door open so hard I was shocked it didn't come off the hinges. I watched her hold her breath as I held mine for more than thirty seconds. When nothing happened and no one spoke, she turned to look at me with a frown.

I shrugged.

Glowering at the presumably empty hallway, Sissily leaned forward still holding onto the door and not stepping a foot outside. "Hello," she whisper-yelled at the empty space and followed it with a loud hiccup. "Great." She muttered on a groan and I had to fight a snicker. Try as she may, she still hiccupped when nervous.

"You okay?" I whispered but her glare made me shut my mouth.

"This is ridiculous, you know?" my best friend hissed and hiccupped once again. "I'm an adult. I can deal with stress without sounding like an idiot."

"Of course, you can," I agreed solemnly.

"I will zap you, Hazel Byrne. Don't patronize me,"

Sissily threatened, so I raised both hands in surrender without a word.

"I meant it, I swear." I bit the inside of my mouth so I didn't laugh when she hiccupped again. "You are a woman, I hear you roar. Rawr." I growled and pawed at the air between us until she cracked a smile. "But you do sound like an idiot with that hiccup," I told her a second before she punched me in the sternum.

"Jackass." With a growl, she also shoved my shoulders when I doubled over, the earlier pain returning with a vengeance. "Lucky there was no one there. We are horrible at staying quiet. Danika knows that. I have no idea why she expects today to be any different."

"It could be because Alex stuck up for me." Pulling the door closed, I moved away from the wall. "She must think I'm finally a responsible adult now."

"You stink like you've lived a month in a whisky barrel, girl. I assure you, she doesn't think you are a responsible anything. The least of all an adult." Waving her hand in front of her face, she scrunched up her nose and stepped away from me.

"Why do you have to kill my dreams, Sissily?" I snickered under my breath when she chortled. "Officially, starting from today, you will be known as a killer of joy."

"I always wanted to have a title." Twining her fingers under her chin, she twirled and blinked rapidly. Shaking my head, I chuckled, flicking a finger between us. "This is why we are friends."

"And because I can drink as much as you can so you don't have to do it alone," she pointed out.

"That, too." Conceding to her wisdom, I bowed and we grinned at each other. "I want to know what they're talking about, too."

"Oh, thank goddess, I thought you'd never say it." Dropping all humor, Sissily snatched my hand and started dragging me toward the door. "If we circle around where the gym and the fighting mats are, I think we can eavesdrop through the vents from the new moon chamber."

"Sissily, you naughty girl." I bared my teeth in a gloating grin. "Who have you sneaked around with so that you know these things? Huh?"

"Mike." She grimaced as she glanced at me over her shoulder.

"Can I kill him now?"

"No."

"You suck." I pouted but at least she smiled.

We were creeping along the large intestine that was the main hallway, circling the coven building like two thieves. Occasionally a jiggling or a clinking sound would rattle from somewhere in the building, the sound echoing along the empty space, making us jump and plaster ourselves to the sides in hopes to make ourselves as small as possible. Magical, smokeless flames danced on top of the sconces attached to the black surface, casting ominous shadows all over the floor and walls that didn't help with our mounting paranoia. Just as I was about to suggest we should turn back, voices trickled from a chamber a few doors down from where we were standing.

Excitement lit up Sissily's face, and I couldn't help but share it. Unease twisted and turned in my gut, but I had to see this through or I would never hear the end of it from my best friend. And she did not need more ammunition to hold over my head, thank you very much.

With a finger pressed to her lips, she led me toward the first door to our right. Latching onto her cold fingers, I followed obediently, cursing myself to high heavens for not picking some flats to wear when I left pack lands. My toes were going numb from placing all my weight on them or I would alert the dead if I stepped on a whole foot in the hallways. Who in their right mind would try to sneak around on four-inch heels? Me. That's who.

Entering the ritual chamber felt foreign to me. It could've been because I knew I was not punished to clean it, as Danika so often made me do, so my mind rebelled when I entered, reminding me that I didn't belong there. But I did belong now. So, I squashed that feeling down with the force of a rhino stomping on glass. I had every right to enter any room in Gatekeeper's coven or any other.

The pentagram on the side of my finger tingled, and Sissily dropped my hand with a tiny squeak, jumping away from me with owlish eyes.

"Ouch." She dragged the sound long enough to be dramatic while shaking her hand like she'd been holding onto live wire.

"Sorry?" I breathed the question and frowned at my hand. I didn't mean to hurt her, if that was what she was accusing me of.

"I don't want to be an anthill, Hazel." Her reference to what occurred to anyone unfortunate enough to be hit by my magic caused her glower to increase. "Watch it."

"I am watching it, you crazy female." Angrily yanking my shoes off one by one, I wiggled one in her face. "I didn't use any magic." A sigh escaped me when my bare feet connected with the cold stone of the floor, and I didn't want to argue anymore. "At least not on purpose. My pentagram tingled though." I scratched at it with my thumb for emphasis.

Sissily cocked her head slightly, a thoughtful expression on her face. When I was about to ask her what she was thinking, she shook her head and motioned for me to follow her to the far corner of the chamber past the simple wooden altar. I wondered how she expected us to know what they were talking about in the other room. Outside of our bickering whispers, the place was as silent as a tomb. You couldn't hear a thing.

My best friend rushed in the corner and dropped on her knees so close to the wall I fully expected her to headbutt it. She expertly maneuvered her body to avoid hurting herself and started poking at the floor with her fingers. Thinking she might need help, I edged closer and kneeled gingerly next to her, holding a hand pressed to my stomach. That damn whisky was ready to punish me for gulping it down instead of savoring it. Acid was bubbling in waves, forming sweat on my hairline and upper lip. That would've been a perfect time to use a refreshing spell if I'd known one. Despite all the power I now had, I was still useless as a witch unless I needed to kill someone, so I pressed my lips together and endured the misery.

"It should pop right off." Sissily kept fidgeting with whatever she was attempting to rip out of the floor.

All I could focus on was holding the contents of my stomach inside and continuing to scratch the pentagram on my finger. Hecate knew it was driving me insane, and I had to prevent myself from screaming in frustration. So, nostrils flaring, I breathed deeply and as slowly as I could. Luckily, I opened my eyes just in time to see Sissily yank something off the floor with such force she pitched backward, the back of her skull aiming right at the cold stone beneath us.

Forgetting all about my nausea, I dived underneath her, so my back took the brunt of the impact with her head. She gasped, but my grunt was low and pained, and I gagged when I tasted acid in my mouth. Taking all of my best friend's weight regardless of how tiny she was pushed all the churning acid up toward my mouth. One of my shoes was also kicked by one of us, I had no idea who did it, and it cluttered toward the altar, breaking the eerie silence.

"We are as quiet as an elephant in a china shop," Sissily hissed, flailing around so she could get herself off me.

I stayed silent because if I tried to say a word, everything was going to spill out of my mouth.

Literally.

All my misery was forgotten when the conversation from the room next to us spilled through. It was coming from the floor. So, curious as a cat, I swallowed thickly and crawled to join my bestie in the corner. When my knee bumped hers, I finally saw what she was struggling with since we entered the chamber. She ripped out the covering from a vent located where the wall met the floor. It sat at a perfect ninety degree angle, and I frowned at it, not understanding why anyone would place a vent there.

"This whole place is weird." I muttered through clenched teeth, still fighting the nausea. "Who puts an air vent in a corner? Idiotic."

Random conversation about the quality of the stone used for the coven building trickled to our ears, but we ignored it, hoping to hear something important if we got lucky.

"It's not an air vent," Sissily said so low I barely heard her.

"Hmm?" When she fully ignored me like I wasn't glaring at the side of her head, I bumped her shoulder with mine. "What?"

"We should be quiet," she mouthed, dramatically shaping each word with her lips like I was a dumbass.

"What did you say?"

With a roll of her eyes at my persistence, she huffed in annoyance. "It's not an air vent," she mumbled and pointed at the now-open hole in the corner of the room.

Curiosity killed the cat, but I leaned forward until my forehead was firmly pressed on the wall, and I peered inside it just as a female voice came through loud and clear as if she were kneeling right next to us.

"Are we going to have the pleasure of meeting your granddaughter, Danika?" The accent was cultured, but it still made the female sound fake and robotic. Almost as if she was faking it just because she wanted to sound sagacious.

My heartbeat picked up and thudded in my ears loud enough to mute whatever answer Danika gave her. Being pressed to the wall the way I was should've helped, but it didn't when the chamber tilted and spun, making me pitch sideways onto Sissily. Both my hands came up to press over my mouth a second too late. The bubbling acid was determined to come out and there was no stopping it. Not wanting to barf all over Sissily, I shoved myself hard with both hands off the wall and twisted in the opposite direction right in time for the projectile vomit to splash all the way to the wooden altar which was sitting unassumingly in the middle of the space.

"Hecate help us." Sissily gasped, but her voice sounded very far away.

My heartbeat was drumming harder, and the pentagram turned from being itchy into trying to burn itself out of my skin. Unfortunately, I was powerless to do anything about it, apart from expelling three more sprays until all the contents of my stomach were on the floor. Silently, I vowed that I would never drink whisky again. Which I rectified and reworded after I had nothing else to eject from my body.

Never was such a long time. A month of staying away from the whisky should be enough to teach it a lesson.

"You okay?" Sissily's voice came in shaky and very close to my ear. Couldn't she smell the vomit? I already wanted to gag again.

"Yeah," I told her on a groan and pushed myself up and away from the mess. That was when I realized that my bestie was holding my hair and tears pricked my eyes. "Thanks."

"Thank me later." The panic, which was the reason her voice sounded shaky, registered in my brain, and my vision cleared immediately when I locked my eyes on her face.

"What's wrong?"

"They're headed here," Sissily rushed to whisper just as we heard the door start to open.

Chapter Five

"Goddess help me, did something die in here?" came a shrill comment from the door as soon as it started to move inward.

We could hear the yapping of people who were crowding at the partially opened entrance of the new moon chamber as we hunkered lower, pressing ourselves as hard as we could to the base of the altar. Must give credit to my best friend, she was fast when she needed to be. The second we realized we were about to get caught, she grabbed my arm and we dove for the altar, thankfully avoiding stepping in the mess I'd made. Curling up around each other, I hoped we were invisible to anyone looking from the door. Sissily's elbow was jabbing me in the soft spot just above the hip bone, but I bit hard on the inside of my mouth so I didn't whimper.

They can't see us. They can't see us. I chanted on repeat inside my head.

"How is this chamber not cleaned?" Danika spoke so

calmly that goosebumps prickled all over the skin of my arms.

I didn't need to be looking at her to know she had her teeth clenched and her nostrils were flaring while she did her best to set the ritual room on fire with her sharp glare. And Hecate help me, I wanted to laugh so hard knowing she was pissed, like I'd never wanted to laugh before. It was immature, but I'd have been lying if I said I didn't want to gloat. That was until I saw a shadow from the corner of my eye and cold sweat washed over me.

One of my shoes was smack in the middle of the chamber, the red sole sticking out like a sore thumb in the all black room.

My eyes nearly popped out of my skull, and I clutched Sissily so hard she pinched my bicep so I would release her.

"Somebody will pay for this." Danika's voice snapped like a whip and I knew in that moment that she saw the shoe as well. It was there, in the tone of her voice, the way she said *somebody*. That amount of disappointment in her words was reserved solely for me. I'd heard it my entire life. "We can continue to my office. I cannot stand the stench."

Everyone followed her while she spoke, and before we knew it, we heard the door close with a loud bang. We both shivered, too afraid to believe we were not discovered. It could've also been from the throb present in the empty space between us. The obsidian which made the walls and floor of the building dulled the sound in a very specific way that it stayed for almost a minute in the empty space, vibrating the air. If the magic flames and black walls and floors didn't spook people enough, the ever-present vibration in the air would do the trick.

"It does stink in here." Sissily's face twisted in such a

grimace, like she smelled rotten cheese. "What in the worlds did you eat, Hazel? Pickled dicks?"

"You're disgusting." Shoving away from her and the stench, which I would never admit was as horrible as she was saying, I hurried to grab my shoes that somehow ended up on two different sides of the altar. "I think Danika saw my shoe. I could feel her death glare aimed at me over the altar."

"We better hurry up and return where she left us. We can pretend we never left the room," my friend suggested reasonably. "How is she going to prove it was us here? Unless she tests DNA on your vomit."

"How many people you know wear five thousand-dollar shoes to come in this building and their name is not Byrne?" Not bothering to wait and see her frown, I hustled to the door and pressed my ear on it.

"As in normal people, or people who like pickled... stuff?" Sissily walked in a wide circle to avoid my mess, and her face was so serious when I glanced at her over my shoulder you could've never guessed she'd just insulted me. Again.

"What is it with you and pickled condiments?" She just twitched her shoulder in a barely there shrug when I glared at her. "And for the record, I drank half a bottle of whisky in less than ten minutes. That's why it stinks. It's all that acidity."

I did feel better after it all came out, though. The itch where the pentagram was on my finger was gone, too. Which reminded me.

"Do you think it's possible that the mark"—my finger popped up in case she didn't know what I was referring to—"warns me when danger is near?" Sissily looked confused, so I let out a huff at my stupidity. "Never mind. It's dumb anyway."

"I never said you were dumb, although you do have some pretty out there ideas most of the time." Her lips twitched in a suppressed smile so she could take the sting out of her words. She was not wrong. "I'm just trying to think of what kind of danger you were in when we came in this chamber. I mean, what are they going to do if they find us eavesdropping? Put us in time out?"

"I'd rather not be found."

"Same. But I'm just saying, you know."

"You are right." With a sigh, I returned to pressing my ear on the door to see if we could leave. "I said it was dumb. It just starts itching or burning at the most inconvenient times, so I thought…I have no clue what I thought."

"It's something to consider." She smacked my shoulder with the back of her hand when I glanced at her incredulously. "I'm serious. You are a riddle for everyone. No one knows what you can, or cannot do. Who's to say that the mark is not guiding you somehow? We should start paying it closer attention and notice when it reacts and why."

"We can go, I think." Pulling the door slowly open, I leaned in only enough to be able to see with one eye down the hallway. No one was there, so I stepped out, waving for Sissily to follow me. "Did you notice that Alex was not with them? Or was it just me?"

"Yeah, I don't think he was with them," she answered reluctantly, probably wondering if she should call me out on changing the subject. I was grateful she dropped it and played along. "Maybe we should take him as an example and skedaddle from here too. We can come back later or tomorrow to talk to Danika. When there are less suits prancing around."

We were about ten feet away from the door when I heard the soft shuffle of feet, and I only had time to grab my friend and push us both flat on the wall face first. Her protest about me mushing her face on the stone died fast when someone cleared their throat too close for me to hope they didn't see us.

"And you see?" I said loud enough for it not to sound like a whisper and waved a hand indicating the wall we were plastered on. "That is the best way to fully feel the vibration of the stone. Your pores absorb its energy when it makes contact with your skin."

Sissily was watching me like she has never seen me before or like I've grown a second head. This girl needed to get with the program because I didn't want Danika to hear I was skulking in the hallways on top of all the rest of the clusterfucks I caused in one day. I wanted to slap my best friend because we were supposed to act like we had a purpose for standing here. No one pays attention if you look like you belong.

Which I thought we were failing at, miserably.

It took everything in me to ignore whoever was standing there watching the show. But Sissily was still silent, gaping like a fish at me.

"Well?" Nodding encouragingly at her, I pointed at the wall she was still leaning on. "Did you feel it?"

"Did I feel what?" she mumbled the question with parted lips.

"The obsidian." Speaking slowly like to a simpleton, I exaggerated the word. "The reason why we are here? Hugging it?"

Instead of catching up, she darted her gaze sideways over my shoulder and right at whoever was standing there silently like some creep. I wanted to turn and see, as well but if I was going to sell the story I had to be committed to it. Otherwise we were doomed. I was a horrible actress.

Sissily snorted.

I really wanted to slap her so she would snap out of it.

"I too would like to know if she felt it," Ace spoke from behind me, laughter evident in his tone. "More importantly, I'd like to know if you felt it, Hazel." I spun around to glower at him so fast I almost tripped. "The vibration, I mean."

Sissily chortled like a fiend.

"You'll feel it all right if you come closer, you snitch." Hissing at him, I pulled my hand back and chucked my shoes at his head. He ducked the fucker. "Why are you here? To get more information to go tell your Alpha? Go. Shoo. He might give you a bone if you are a good boy."

"You're such a bitch," Sissily muttered under her breath, shaking her head and giving Ace a pitying glance.

"It's one of her charms, Sissily. Don't be too upset with her." Grinning from ear to ear, the shifter told her, unperturbed by my jab.

"He could've said something instead of letting me make a fool out of myself and lurking there without a word." If I sounded defensive, it was because I was. I was still salty that he called Alex and told him about the skirmish that morning.

"I wanted to see what happens next." Ace shrugged unapologetically and shoved his hands in the pockets of his jeans. "It was quite impressive, really. You should audition sometimes. You might become a star for the humans."

"If you laugh, I'll zap you." I pointed at Sissily who was about to do just that. "And you…"

"Hey, hey, I come in peace." The moment my finger pointed in his direction, Ace raised both hands, palms up in surrender. "Alex seems very unhappy about something that was said, which is why he told them he had some urgent pack business to attend to and left. He told me to find you, and not let you out of my sight." Determination shone in his irises and chills skirted up my spine when his wolf peeked at me through them. "Something is off about this whole visit, Hazel. Like it or not, you are stuck with me until Alpha says you are free."

Self-preservation was a new hobby of mine so forgetting all jabs and tormenting of the shifter, I hugged my middle and leaned back on the wall. Both of them fully expected me to argue about having a bodyguard with me twenty-four seven, but I was no longer the dumb Hazel from a few weeks ago. I'd learned my lesson the hard way. This Hazel was the obedient one.

Well, obedient-ish.

Let's not go too far.

"Did he say why?" Sissily immediately shuffled up to me and wrapped an arm over my shoulders. "Should we stay here or leave, you think?" Her palm started rubbing my shoulder and I appreciated the support and the warmth it created over my chilled skin.

Ace shook his head and cautiously turned to check behind him and down the hallway to make sure we were the only ones here. "The only thing he said was trust no one and the only way you are separated from Hazel better be by removing your dead carcass from her."

"That sounds ominous." I visibly shivered. "Maybe we should leave and come back tomorrow. I mean I already told Danika why I was here. If she agrees to my plan, she knows my number."

"We go back to pack lands," Ace agreed too happily, the relief evident on his face.

"Actually, I haven't felt like a normal person since this crazy shit show started. I think we should go have a good cup of coffee and some pastries." I waved a hand to stop the shifter's protests. "Amber will be there. Plus, that café is as good as pack lands, don't you think?"

"It's too much of a risk," he started, and lo and behold, Sissily decided to come to my rescue.

"She was sick earlier, and her stomach is empty right now. Plus, she'll be less of a pain in the ass if we feed her and load her with caffeine."

"I told you not to gulp that whisky down like that," Ace lectured, so I narrowed my eyes on him.

"Okay, Dad. I'll sip it slower next time." The crooked grin he gave me used to flip flop my stomach, but I was still too woozy to react. "Scratch that. Me and Mr. Whisky are taking a break. It's not me, it's him."

"I bet it is." Sissily snickered, so I bumped her with my shoulder.

"Okay, okay." Ace took a step backward, sounding defeated. "You two win. Let's take you for a coffee and some food. Let Amber deal with your spoiled asses. Bloody witches. Never happy with anything you want to do."

"Keep talking and I'll turn you into a frog," Sissily threatened with a huge smile. Ever since they'd stuck me in a room at Alex's house, these two had become as thick as thieves.

"I'll willingly sacrifice myself if Hazel kisses me after it."

"Kiss you?" Taking his lead to lighten the mood, we followed behind him. "If she turns you into a frog, I'll eat you."

The shifter's eyebrows shot up all the way to his hairline, and Sissily choked next to me.

"I meant I'll fry your drumsticks, fool." Glaring at his excited face, I elbowed my best friend for good measure. "The two of you are horrible."

Ace bent down and picked up the shoes I'd thrown at him without slowing his stride. Both of them kept snorting and choking while I stewed in frustration.

"Whatever you say, princess." Ace snickered, not knowing how blessed he was for holding my shoes in his hands. If I'd had them, I would've jabbed the heel in the back of his skull.

"Just hurry up. Nut job." Shaking my head, I ignored their shenanigans.

"We wasted precious time sneaking around and coming here. We didn't hear any useful information," Sissily mumbled as she rubbernecked to make sure no one was watching us leave.

"Not necessarily true," I pointed out, watching Ace lift his nose and sniff the air. He was making sure no one was hiding around us. "I learned that the ritual chambers have air vents tucked in the corners." Incredulously, I shook my head, still baffled by that discovery.

"Not all chambers, just that one," Sissily corrected me, but she stiffened at my mention of the duct she opened so we could eavesdrop. "And it's not an air vent."

"What else could it be, Sissily?"

"It's a drain, not a vent." Her tone was short, and I frowned at her, my curiosity peaked.

"A drain for water when they clean the floors you mean?" When she stayed silent and stared ahead as if we were facing a horseman of the apocalypse, I tugged on her arm. "A drain for water?"

"No."

"You have to give me more than that. I won't stop until you tell me." She knew it; I knew it, too. I spoke the truth.

"For blood," Sissily rushed the word, hoping I wouldn't hear it.

I tripped over my own two feet.

Chapter Six

After a quick shower and a visit to my store size closet at Danika's house, I was tucked into the back seat of Ace's SUV with my eyes closed, listening to him and Sissily bicker about some band. I'd been tense and on the edge for so long, it was taking a huge toll on me. Emotionally more than any other way. Every night I literally passed out the second my head would hit the pillow but I woke up every morning more exhausted than when I went to bed.

My head rolled to the side and I lifted my arm to look at my skin. The sigils that were covering every inch of it and conveniently turned me into a glowstick were nowhere in sight. Whatever juju Danika did to make them invisible to anyone else didn't work on me, so I knew they were gone for real. At least for the time being.

Not like I was complaining or anything.

But I did kinda get used to them.

"I could kill for a Danish." Sissily twisted in the passenger seat to wiggle her eyebrows at me. The more adversity we faced, the more she came out of her shell. She was no longer constantly serious or stoic.

"I just need coffee." Eyes slightly opened so I could see her through my lashes, I pressed a hand over my belly. "Anything more than that might cause more trouble than it's worth it."

"Maybe you'll learn one of these days to stay away from drinking early in the morning."

"Can you imagine Danika's face when she walked into that chamber?" Ace just shook his head at our snickering like two-year-old's before I was finished talking. "Just by her tone, I pictured it scrunched up like she sucked on a rotten lemon."

"She'll make us pay for it," Sissily threw at Ace as a justification for our immaturity. "This one"—her thumb pointed at me over her shoulder—"sprinkled her shoes around the ritual room like breadcrumbs. A blind person could see them."

"Yeah, she knew it was us." I agreed unperturbed.

The city was passing by as I stared limply through the window as office buildings and stores blurred into a never-ending line of splattered watercolors on the canvas of life. My butt slid across the leather seat when Ace took a sharp turn on East street as he tried to beat the red light.

"If you want, I can drive," Sissily sassed him, insulting his driving skills in a nice way.

"I'm good, thanks," was Ace's drawled reply, and I just rolled my eyes.

"I still want to know why Alex Velcro-ed you to my ass, Ace." Twisting my leg to the side, I leaned in slightly so I could admire the Michael Kors flats I had on. They were among the cheapest shoes I own, and I figured if we got attacked—which in my life was a ninety percent possibility—and they got ruined, I'd be able to replace them easily.

"Me too." He growled low in his throat, and when I looked up, I found him looking at me through the rearview mirror.

"I mean we can ask…"

"No," Ace cut me off sharply, and I glared at him.

"Don't you dare bark commands at me, shifter. I'm not pack, so I don't have to deal with your attitude. I'll stick an umbrella in your mouth and open it."

"She learned that one from me," Sissily announced, proudly preening on the passenger seat like a peacock.

Ace glanced at me then at Sissily with such a serious face it rendered me mute because it was very uncharacteristic of him.

"The two of you are the strangest females I have met in my life," he decided to tell us after he parked the cumbersome SUV in a paid parking garage before jumping out so he could open the doors for us. "Don't get me wrong, but I'm starting to think that witches have some screws loose up here." His thick finger tapped on the side of his temple.

"You think it's maybe all that magic we channel?" Sissily looked so earnest when she spoke that I almost believed she was asking a genuine question.

Ace gave her a cursory up and down then shook his head." Nah, I think it's just the two of you that are weirdos; you were dropped on your heads when you were born."

Seeing the coffee shop across the street as we exited the parking garage had me salivating. My stomach was eating itself already since it had been empty for hours at that point. Leaving Sissily and Ace to snark at each other, I quickened my step, ready to jaywalk across so I could get to it faster. I also needed one of those hugs I knew was waiting for me the moment Amber saw me. I'd never admit it to anyone, but every time that female wrapped her arms around me, I wanted to cry.

There was no deception, no manipulation, scorn or expectation in her action. It was just that. A simple hug to show that you mattered to her. And it made me crack like an eggshell and bleed inside for all those times I'd needed it but was denied by Danika because showing emotion was weakness. I was also worried about River. It'd been more than a week but he was not awake yet.

I was hoping Amber had some news about that, too.

A blaring of a horn had me jumping back and barely avoiding being mowed down in the middle of the street by a crappy KIA with a sticker at the back that said "I'm a baby, and I'm aboard." Heart galloping wildly in my ribcage, I clutched my chest with one hand and after confirming no one was staring at me, sent a string of magic to the left back tire. It was satisfactory when it popped and the person driving jerked the wheel to the side, effectively nailing themselves at a parked vehicle.

"I bet *baby* is aboard and crying right now." Shooting daggers at the brunette that came out flailing her arms, I breathed deeply and continued toward the beckoning glass door of the café.

"What are you doing?" Sissily materialized next to me and hissed the question while grabbing me under the arm and manhandling me across the street.

"I was walking." Wiggling to try and escape her grip while trying to look normal and not like a toddler throwing a tantrum was difficult. A guy was looking at us strangely from two shops down, so I gave up my struggle with my best friend and cocked an eyebrow at his judgmental stare. "Can I help you?"

"It's your fault that lady almost hurt herself," the dude had the audacity to holler at me as he pointed at the KIA that nearly ran me over.

One glance in that direction made me do a double take because dozens of people had gathered around it and everyone was arguing, while the *baby aboard* was clutching her head, pretending like she was about to faint although no one was paying her attention.

I frowned.

"Seriously, Hazel, you need to cut that shit out. You can't treat people like trash," Sissily snapped and grabbed my upper arm, shoving me toward the café.

Stunned, I stumbled to the sidewalk, confused to no end. What in the worlds was happening? And where the hell did Ace go? Craning my neck, I looked around for the shifter while keeping an eye on my best friend in case she decided to get physical again. Something was not right, I just couldn't put my finger on it.

"Sissily, where is Ace?" I took a few steps away so I could keep the distance between us when she joined me on the sidewalk.

"Cleaning up your mess. It's all any of us do anymore," she told me so harshly I literally stumbled back as if she'd landed a physical blow. "What? You don't like hearing the truth, Miss Perfect?"

"She is responsible for everything." The guy that gave me a piece of his mind a minute ago shouted above the rest so he could be heard. "She couldn't use the crosswalk. The poor lady almost killed herself to avoid her."

While focused on my best friend, I had not realized that a group had started forming around us, all of them with scrunched up faces and pointed fingers. Unease spread through me, and the moment I spotted Ace next to the brunette arguing with random humans, it redoubled. Rubbernecking up and down the street confirmed my suspicions that all the yelling and shouting was not natural. Seeing Sissily staring pointedly at my hand made me look down too so I could find myself scratching at the pentagram marking so hard I made my finger bleed.

Something was causing all of this. They used the near miss with the vehicle to fuel an angry mob crying for blood, including my best friend.

My blood.

"Sissily, listen to me." It was not easy to get her attention, but she finally locked gazes with me after I repeated myself three times. "This is not you. Something is going on, and I need your help to fix it."

"Aren't you the strongest witch there is?" She sneered, and although I knew this was not her, it still stung like a bitch. "Fix it yourself."

Her eyes latched onto my bleeding finger again. And she licked her lips.

My heart skipped a beat.

"I'm trying." Hoping to keep her focused on talking to me, my gaze darted around, watching the angry humans close up around us. "That's why I need you to pinch yourself. A spell or someone is making you feel that anger. You need to snap out of it because I need your help."

"What?" Looking at me like I'd grown a second head, she took a step closer. "For once, take responsibility when you fuck up, Hazel. You can't always blame it on others."

Hearing that made me see red. Sissily, out of all people, should have known me better than that. Spell or not I really wanted to slap her. So, as my best friend took another step closer while focused solely on my bleeding hand I slid the rest of the distance between us and, pulling my hand back, I slapped her as hard as I could.

Her head was flung to the side, making her ponytail fly in an arc and end up on the side of her face instead of the back of her skull. With a gasp, she cupped the stinging cheek that had red fingers imprinted on it and leaned forward, using me to keep herself from falling. Taking hold of her shoulders, I helped her regain her balance and I shoved her behind me so that she was between me and the coffee shop. The humans were too close and looked ready to attack.

"Bitch. Grab her. It's her fault. She did it on purpose. I saw her; she tried to kill the poor lady." Angry voices attempted to out-shout each other. The twisted faces of humans full of rage were blurring in front of me.

Angry.

They were all so angry.

And that's when it dawned on me.

"Anger demon," I called out over my shoulder, praying to Hecate slapping Sissily had done the trick to wake her from the effect. "Did you hear me?"

"The dead at the cemetery outside of Cleveland heard you, too. Not just me," she deadpanned, sounding unimpressed.

Making a quick turn, I shoved my bleeding finger in her face and made her recoil away from me. "Oh, good. It actually worked."

"You mean to tell me you slapped me like I owed you something and you had no idea that it would work?"

"You owe me plenty of things, and I haven't slapped you before," I pointed out. "We have a bigger problem, however. They are about ready to pounce and I have no clue where the Anger demon is."

"If you look, I'll hold them back." Having my best friend back was a relief like nothing else. Plus, her teeth were clenched and she was shaking her arms in preparation. Sissily was pissed so I felt slightly sad for the humans.

"Be nice, Sissily. It's not their fault." Climbing a low wall built to protect the floor to ceiling window of the café, I stood on my tiptoes so I could better see where the demon was hiding. This particular demon's power only worked if they had a visual of their victims at all times. So he, or she, had to be near. I just had to find them. Instead of finding the culprit of all my current troubles, my eyes locked on Ace and my heart punched at the roof of my mouth. My mouth opened so I could warn Sissily but nothing came out apart from a pathetic squeak.

My bestie was busy too, pulling her arms back and throwing them forward with a forceful wind that was knocking humans on their asses. On the bright side, she was not harming them, so I held onto that silver lining. Swallowing thickly, I tried warning her again.

"Ace is furious and he's about to shift in broad daylight." The words came out rushed and shaky. My tone was all wobbly because my heart was beating in my throat.

"He wouldn't." Sissily pushed through clenched feet and shoved the group of humans back a few steps.

"Actually, I think he totally would." As Ace started transforming, I watched, mesmerized and horrified at the same time. "And he's doing it. Super weird."

"Oh, shit." She saw him, and her eyes widened. "You know what? Screw the demon. When I tell you, grab Ace and we are out of here."

She didn't give me time to agree or disagree. Lifting her right arm up in the air, she spread her fingers and lightning streaked across the sky that was turning from bright blue to dark gray in seconds. The moment the second lightning touched the tips of her fingers, she threw her other hand in front of her and the lightning passed through her, only to imbed itself in the middle of the angry mob. Good thing the demon could only make them angry, not stupid. All of them dispersed, running in all directions.

"Now" Sissily screamed and I dashed to Ace, wrapping both arms around him. With everything in me I sort of tackled him toward the door of the café which only worked since he was too busy trying to shift instead of shaking me off like a flea. Sissily joined me and all three of us tumbled inside Amber's cafe with the merry jingling of the bell above the door.

Chapter Seven

"Look what the wolf dragged in." Amber spoke from right above us while we were a tangled mess of limbs on the floor. Her red corkscrews circled her face like a halo as she leaned over us to check for injuries.

I couldn't just get up to get my hug because I had to help Ace who was shaking his head adamantly, but thankfully he was no longer shifting. He was, however, pale like he'd seen a ghost, and I was worried that he might get sick.

"Why are all of you not angry?" asked Amber while holding Ace up by his shoulders. "There is an Anger demon outside causing a riot on the street."

"Is that what that all was?" Ace rasped and leaned forward on one arm to cough out whatever was clogging his throat.

"We have wards around the shop. This has been going on the last two or three hours. The moment I caught what was happening, I called Alex and told him to keep everyone away from here. Especially himself. We closed the shop too." Amber kneeled next to Ace, rubbing his back soothingly. "If you're still fighting the shift I can call him to command you, but he cannot come here. Not now, or we will have much bigger problems than a measly Anger demon."

"I'm okay." The shifter wheezed, still gulping air like he'd run a marathon.

Since I knew she would take better care of the shifter than I would, I slid my butt closer to Sissily, who was sitting mutely on the café floor just inside the door, staring into space. My best friend looked so dejected that my heart twisted painfully in my chest. The moment I slung my arm around her shoulders, she tipped over and tucked her head on my chest. It took a lot to make Sissily show emotions like this in public, so it spoke volumes about our mental state. We were all drained.

"I'm a horrible person," Sissily muttered into my shirt.

"We already knew that. Why are you announcing it like it's a revelation?" My attempt at humor made her lift her head to give me a flat look. "What? Too soon?"

"You're not helping." She wiggled her arm. "Rub my arm to make me feel better." With a roll of my eyes, I pressed my palm to her bicep. "Not too hard," she immediately complained.

"Yes, ma'am." Obediently, I did what she asked while she wallowed in guilt for saying mean things to me. We both knew it wasn't her fault, but I more than anyone could understand where she was coming from.

Things sometimes stayed imprinted on your conscience.

"As much as I hate to say it, I think we need to call Danika." The silence following my statement confirmed that everyone felt the same way when it came to my grandmother. However, she was a necessary evil in the situation. "Or"—since everyone was looking at me, I shrugged like it was not a big deal—"I could go and deal with it."

"Absolutely not," Ace snarled from where he was still kneeling on the floor. "I promised I wouldn't let you out of my sight, and if I go back out there again, there is no stopping the shift. My wolf will see only blood if that rage I felt consumes him."

"Use your inside voice, Ace," I spoke sweetly, giving the glaring shifter a sugary smile full of teeth. "I don't need permission, I was just stating the options we have."

"We could wait it out," Amber suggested. "I already called this in after I warned Alex. The coven is notified."

"And no one is here yet," I said as Sissily and I looked at each other.

"Alex mentioned delegations visiting your grandmother." As much as Amber wanted to seem like she was not concerned, her twisting one strand of hair around her finger over and over told a different story. "Oh dear. You're bleeding."

As she rushed toward me, I lifted my hand to see what she was talking about. At first, I thought I got hurt when we shouldered our way in, but what she was worrying about was my bleeding hand.

"Ah, that's nothing, Amber. I scratched myself there."

"How did you catch on that it's an Anger demon, Hazel?" Sissily suddenly perked up. At my confusion, she pointed at the hand I had up between me and Amber. "Did you snap out of it because you made yourself bleed? Was that it?"

"Ummm." Frowning at the mark, I thought about it for a long moment. Was that why I was myself and not as rage-filled as the rest of them? "I don't think so? I mean, I was never really angry. Annoyed, yes. That the two of you kept bickering. But never really at a point where I wanted to hurt or insult you."

Sissily grimaced at the reminder, but I simply shrugged. I was not reminding her to be an ass, I was simply stating facts. Maybe she had something there because I couldn't remember when I started scratching the mark. As a matter of fact, I couldn't remember it being itchy on the way to the café or after that either.

"She may not be affected at all." Ace, who finally took control of himself, was now sitting with his legs bent at the knees, leaning back on his arms. "I saw when she was nearly hit by that car, which swerved her way on purpose. She was freaked out, and she busted the tire, but it was a typical Hazel move and attitude."

"What's that supposed to mean?" I glowered at him, and he raised both eyebrows as if to say touché. "Whatever." I hated when he was right. "That assumption"—I glanced at him pointedly—"only confirms that I should go and find the demon. If this has been reported to the coven and yet here we are wondering what to do, I think the message is clear. They are not coming."

"I'd like to say that it's a bad idea, but I'm afraid I'd have to agree with Hazel." Amber reluctantly backed me up when the other two immediately started arguing. "I trust she will do the right thing and not act recklessly." Taking hold of both my hands, she made sure I had my gaze locked on hers. "It would destroy me to have her hurt, too. Watching over River is hard enough, I don't think I could handle something happening to both of you."

"Is…" I couldn't finish the question because of the fist size lump that formed in my throat. From the corner of my eye, I watched Ace look away from us, and Sissily duck her head.

"Nothing yet." Amber shook her head sadly, squeezing my fingers in a silent support.

"I smudged you with blood." Clearing my throat and changing the subject, I whipped her dirty hand off my pants and laughed when she looked at me with a horrified expression on her face. "It's okay."

"How is it okay to do that with pants that cost more than what this shop makes in a week?" Recoiling from me, she rushed to grab a towel and returned to clean up the fabric. "Amber, it's okay…"

"I know it's okay; I just need to do something so I don't start fretting about you leaving the shop and going out there." She muttered under her breath while scrubbing rigorously on my pants and throwing anxious glances at the floor to ceiling window and the fights breaking out everywhere.

"If I tie something around my leg, a fork maybe that would stab me every step I take, I might be able to withstand the influence," Sissily suggested hopefully. "I'm not sitting here while Hazel is out there in that mob."

"She's not going anywhere without me, so…" Ace shrugged unapologetically, daring me to say something.

Wisely I kept my mouth shut but only because I could see his wolf peeking through his irises. He was still struggling with the shift and we had enough trouble as it was without adding that to the mix.

One day. Was that too much to ask? Just one day where I stepped out of that damn room and the world didn't go to shit.

"I can control my magic now. For the most part." I muttered that last part under my breath. "All I need to do is find the demon, knock his lights out, bag him, and come back."

"Right." Sissily droned on in a flat tone.

"It's an Anger demon, Sissily. I mean, how hard could it be?" Taking hold of Amber's hands, I stepped away before she ripped my pants. There was barely any fabric left from her scrubbing. "It would've been helpful to know in which general direction the bastard was hiding, but I'll figure it out."

It dawned on me then about Alex's warning to Ace. "Do you think this is what Alex was worried about when he told you not to leave me out of your sight?"

"Don't know, don't care." Pushing himself up, he straightened and stretched both arms over his head. Even disheveled the way he was, the shifter was perfect eye candy. "If you've made up your mind to go, lead the way."

"You're right." Moving around Amber, I walked up to him and took his hand. "There is no way you'll let me out of your sight."

"Damn right." He nodded, a line forming between his eyebrows while he watched me hold his hand. "What…"

"Sorry." My magic trickled through my fingers into his, and he stiffened from the electrical current I was pushing at him.

"Hazel, no," Sissily shrieked as she scrambled up and rushed to where we were standing.

Afraid I might accidentally hurt him, I slipped a hand behind his head and stopped the magic flow the second his eyes rolled back. With the help of Sissily—who made it to us just in time—we lowered him on the floor. I'd be lying if I said that I was not internally freaking out until I saw his chest rise and fall. I'd never done that before, but I had no doubt it would work.

After our crazy trip to Hell and back I learned that lesson.

Lesson 17: *Everything you resist will turn your life upside down. To win in life you need to embrace the unthinkable. Like being a dud with ancient power ready to make itself known to the worlds.*

"He's okay." Guiltily, I glanced at Amber over my shoulder. "He's going to have a killer headache, but he's okay."

"You could've hurt him." My best friend slapped me with the back of her hand.

"You sure developed a gift for stating the obvious, girl." Annoyed, I stood up from where I was crouched next to Ace. "You think it would've been better if he followed me outside? He would've hurt a human or worse, he would've killed someone. You think Ace will be able to live with himself if he hurt an innocent?"

"That was smart, Hazel." Amber spoke, but she was not looking at us. She was staring at the rioting crowd outside. "Thank you for taking care of our pack. Pack males act all tough in front of the outsiders, but we know better. They are kind and honorable deep inside."

A loud growl broke the silence after her words, and my face heated up as I pressed a hand over my belly. With everything going on, I'd totally forgotten how hungry I was, but using a bit of magic at the street and on Ace in the café just added to the mounting gurgling in my gut.

"I hate to ask..."

But Amber was already in motion like this was the one task she was born to do. Her entire demeanor changed from melancholy to full of energy. "I have just the thing, ladies. We baked a lot of stuff before the problems started and we had to lock up the shop. I had a horrible feeling since we opened, so I sent the two girls home before the shouting exploded into...well, this. I was going to pack up all the food and take it home for everyone, but you two should have first picks."

Sissily and I were inching closer while she fussed around behind the counter, and the moment she slid the glass door of the display and waved us in, we fell on the pastry like rabies infected raccoons on steroids.

"Tfank fu," I mumbled with a mouth full of a blueberry muffin. "Itf delifious."

My best friend swallowed half a Danish without chewing and laughed out loud at the breadcrumbs spraying from my lips. "If she wasn't an animal, she would've said thank you, it's delicious."

Amber was grinning from ear to ear like a proud mama bear while we stuffed our faces for a good five minutes. Slowly the weakness tugging on my shoulders and spine dissipated and I felt better than I had in weeks. Sissily was munching on a cherry Danish, happily humming a tune only she could understand when I caught Amber's attention and tried my best to relay what I was planning to do. Much to my surprise, she leaned forward and tucked my best friend in a one arm hug.

Reaching for Sissily's hand, I squeezed her fingers in apology before zapping her with a current of my magic. She stiffened, dropping her half eaten Danish with a splat at our feet before sagging in Amber's arms.

"Sorry," I told my unconscious friend.

"I'll take care of her, go." Amber pulled Sissily firmly to her body and walked her around the counter toward the plush armchairs at the end of the café.

"I'll be back as fast as I can." Sticking a croissant in my mouth, I grabbed one more in my hand as I started for the door. My free hand was on the doorknob when Amber called out to me.

"And, Hazel. Don't make me regret thinking this was a great idea. You come back alive, you hear me?"

"You mean unharmed, right?"

"No." She let out a snorting laugh, and her eyes danced with mischief when they locked on mine. "The demon can take a limb for all I care, we can work with that. Be banged up all you want, just come back alive. I can fix alive."

Gulping down all the emotions that were trying to choke me, I did something I would've never done before. Darting back inside, I threw my arms around her and hugged her so tight like my life depended on it. On a sigh, she wrapped me in her embrace and rocked us from side to side for a long moment.

"Thank you," I whispered in her hair that smelled like vanilla and coconut.

"Sweet girl." Petting my hair, she finally pushed me at arm's length. "You have no idea how much you are loved." A tear trickled down my cheek, and she wiped it away with a secretive smile. "Alex and I wouldn't know what to do without you anymore."

Blowing air multiple times through pursed lips so I didn't break down crying in the middle of the café, I nodded at her. "Alive. Right. I can do that."

"You better, Hazel Byrne. Don't make me come out there looking for you. You won't like what happens." The stern words were softened by her smiling face.

"Jack has told me all about it. I wouldn't dream of it."

I walked out of the café with Amber's laugh still ringing in my ears. I only hoped I didn't lie to the one person that had treated me like she was my mother since I'd known her. My soul would not have peace if I ever hurt Amber.

Chapter Eight

It took me a good ten minutes to duck under swinging fists, twist away from kicks and grabs for my hair. Out on the street was brutal. Inside the shop, the sound was mostly muted, so we couldn't hear the blood curdling screams, animalistic shrieks and snarls echoing off the tall buildings. It was hard to believe these were humans arguing and fighting.

"Where do you think you're going?"

So lost in my disbelief that they would turn into this when influenced by the demon, I didn't see the tall man who stepped in front of me until it was too late. Knowing my luck, the human couldn't have been a tiny scrawny accountant type of a person. No. I got the gym enthusiast that had arms so beefed up I bet he couldn't wipe his own ass.

"Me?" Acting scared, I batted my eyelashes at him. I'm trying to hide from all the bad people." Hoping he would fall for it and leave me be was too much to ask. The moment I was about to circle around him, he grabbed a handful of my hair.

"Ah, fuck." I hissed when my skull was lit on fire from the way he was pulling. "I really"—taking hold of his beefy arm I used it as leverage to swing myself in the air and kick him in the head. He immediately released my poor strands —"didn't want to hurt you."

He dropped like a rock at my feet along with a few chunks of my tresses, but I couldn't mingle longer unless I wanted to deal with more of those. On a whim, I darted left when I exited the café, hoping to go as far as the angry mob had reached. My plan was to look for the demon on the outskirts of the affected area. From what I'd read back when I was hoping that I'd be a great witch one day, Anger demons were easily recognized because you felt absolute rage when they were near. Since I was not affected by the bastard, I had no idea how I would pin down who it was.

My heart skipped a beat when two barrel chested humans circled a young woman and her three children. Without realizing what I was doing, my feet were eating up the space across the street before I froze mid-step. The oldest of the three children, age twelve or so by the looks of it, picked up a piece of a broken brick by his feet that I hadn't noticed until then. With a screech of a banshee, he jumped on one of the humans and started bashing his head with it. The other two children followed their brother and latched onto the man's legs and began biting.

The second human didn't know what to do, and while he gaped at his buddy, he didn't see the woman yanking her high heel off her foot and swinging it at his head. His scream made the hairs on the back of my neck stand on end, so I missed that I was standing in the middle of a busy street with people yelling at each other, arguing and fighting.

The hit to the back of my head came as a surprise.

"Sonofab..." Stumbling forward, I threw my hand back with intention to block if another hit was coming.

My magic, however, didn't get the memo, so I heard the screech of the person when my power slammed into them. Eyes watering, I blinked behind me to see if I'd killed the human only to be shocked with a whole bunch of them staring at me with open mouths. The one who hit me in the head was crumpled on the ground, but from what I could see was still breathing.

"Ummm..." I had no idea what to say.

"Witch!" somebody thundered from my open-mouthed audience, and I cringed when the rest of them joined in, their eyes bloodshot and crazed.

They all moved as one, hunching their shoulders and ready to chase me. I didn't wait to find out if I could fight my way out of it. Spinning on my heel, I bolted like the wind away from all of them.

"That will teach you"—I huffed and gasped as I ran—"to go help others when you can't even help yourself."

When I turned a corner and saw an alley within reach before the mob could get to me, I took the chance. Ducking in the narrow passage, I slowed down my pace so my feet smacking the concrete didn't give away my hiding place. Buildings towered over it on both sides, forming deep shadows good enough to conceal my presence. So halfway in the alley, I plastered myself to the wall near two trash containers. Heart hammering in my throat, I had to flare my nostrils to drag as much air as I could so I didn't gasp and give my hiding place away.

Maybe I should have been more like Danika. She

would've blasted the lot of them with magic without blinking an eye. My grandmother would not lose sleep over hurt humans. I, on the other hand, had taken care of them for most of my life and had no intention of stopping now. One angry mob was not going to change my mind.

Shouts and hoots came from the mouth of the alley, and I watched as much as I could as the river of people ran past it, chasing after their own rage. I was no longer leading that sprint, yet they continued as if they could still see me in front of them. My leg began bouncing while I waited, impatience crowding my every thought.

I needed to stop messing around and find the demon. Who knew how long Ace and Sissily would be out? Worse than being the reason for an actual witch hunt was to be the reason your friends got hurt. Or hurt others. So the moment the last chaser hooted and dashed after the rest, I inched closer to the street, tiptoeing my way to the entrance of the alley.

If it weren't for my personal witch hunt, I never would've seen him.

About five foot eleven tall, with plain features, unassuming t-shirt and jeans and dirty brown hair, the demon was…well, the best way to describe it was, forgettable. How I knew it was the Anger demon was very simple and uneventful, too. He had his hands in his pockets and a shit eating grin as he strolled leisurely behind the running humans.

Ducking my head out of the alley a few times in a row to check that no one was going to ambush me the second I stepped foot out, I narrowed my eyes on the bastard. The fury I felt building in my chest had nothing to do with the demon's power but everything to do with him. I wanted to rip him apart limb from limb.

The last time I had a psychic encounter with my power it wanted me to trust it and follow my instincts. If I fought it, it'd work against me. If I followed its lead, it would work in my best interest. That was fine and dandy until you realized that what was good for the spider was chaos for the fly. I had to trust it this time, though. As long as I played along I could somewhat control it.

I stepped out of the alley.

The demon's head snapped in my direction instantly. The grin that had stretched his mouth unnaturally, showing way too many teeth, slipped, but mine grew. While he took my measure, I carefully closed the distance between us.

"Fancy meeting you here," I remarked conversationally, doing my best to look as unthreatening as possible.

Cocking his head to the side, he narrowed his black eyes on my hand just as the pentagram started burning as if wanting to get itself out of my skin. "A witch," he hissed, his accent so strange it took me a second to get what he said.

"And a demon walk into a bar." When he snarled at me, I lifted both hands in the air, palms up. "You don't like jokes. Got it."

"You think this is funny, witch?" Taking a step toward me, he slightly hunched over and that was my queue.

"Nope." I made the popping sound with my lips just to annoy him. "But this might be."

Since my hands were still in the air and my palms were facing him, I gave up the control I had to constantly maintain on my magic. It was like holding a hand over a hose while the water was trying to push through. Now that I'd removed that obstacle, my power rushed out, ready to play. Much to my surprise, my skin lit up as all the sigils reappeared on every inch of it.

The demon widened his pitch-black eyes and tried to run.

Poor thing had no idea there was no escape for him—or me—where my magic was concerned.

Strong winds picked up, lashing my hair around my face, and I felt my feet lift off the ground. Thick strings of magic like rope burst out of my palms and wrapped around the demon's limbs. It told me that whatever type of magic this was, it was always listening to my thoughts. I should've thought of no drama and problems instead of ripping limbs from demons.

Fighting for his life, the demon roared his frustration and pulled on the ropes of power that were restraining him with everything he had. Not expecting him to be that powerful, I threw my head back and screamed when his yanking on my magic felt like he was trying to rip my torso apart. I wanted to ask him questions about why he was here and who told him it was okay to attack humans, but all my good intentions went down the drain when I felt pain like never before.

"No, you don't," I pushed through clenched teeth and added my own intent and strength to the power streaming out of me.

I almost had him, I could see his arms ready to pop out of his shoulders when the angry mob leading the witch hunt joined us on the street. When they saw us standing in the middle—well the demon standing and me levitating a foot off the ground—they bellowed as one and beelined for us.

The bastard was using the humans to help him escape.

I needed a new strategy.

Stopping the streams of power that held the demon from escaping, I dropped on one knee on the asphalt. Falling forward on one hand fooled the demon into believing that I couldn't maintain the magic, so he hissed and jumped at me, sharp claws forming at his fingertips. The ground was vibrating from the thundering footsteps of the angry mob, but I was focused on something else. All the roots and living things that were beneath it. I called on them to come and aid me. The demon was almost on top of me, his shadow falling over me like a blanket of doom.

A sharp claw sunk inside my shoulder as the demon grabbed me, lifting his other arm up ready to rip me to shreds. Calm came over me, and instead of crying out at the pain, I lifted my head up fully to look at his rage twisted face.

That was when the concrete under my hand split open and roots as thick as cables slithered from under it. Multiple ones speared through the demon's upper body, and I would never forget the utter shocked expression on his face. Mine could've looked the same because I watched as black tendrils spread over the demon's skin and burst through it, effectively shredding him alive.

Hot blood sprayed all over me when he burst like a balloon, his final cry echoing in my ears. I stayed like that for a long moment, not believing what had just happened when I realized it was too quiet on the street. Slowly, I turned my head to the side.

A wall of people stood there dazed and stunned, and a little afraid, watching me like they were seeing an alien. Not that I blamed them but I fidgeted where I was kneeling, uncomfortable from all the staring. A slow clapping broke the awkward silence, and my head snapped in that direction.

Danika stood on the street, on the opposite side of the wall of humans. On either side of her stood a person dressed in all black, a male on the right and a female on the left. The only difference between the two was the gold and silver pins they wore on their ties. The female was clapping with a gleeful grin on her face while Danika looked like she was made of stone. Only her emerald eyes were flashing with fury, destroying the calm façade.

"How marvelous!" The female laughed. "You've been holding out on us, Danika. Your grandchild is perfect."

"Fuck my life," I breathed and closed my eyes.

Chapter Nine

"I'm sorry," I mumbled under my breath to Sissily who sat next to me in the torture chairs in Danika's office and refused to even look at me much less talk.

She also refused to let me go to the coven alone, thank the goddess.

Around us, murmured whispers buzzed like a cloud of bees, and I fidgeted in the stupid chair because I could feel their eyes on me. Ace was kind enough to inform me that my sigils were not visible to any of the newcomers. I made him ask before I was able to breathe a sigh of relief.

Another thing that made me terribly uncomfortable was the way Danika spoke to the few witches crowded around her, but she kept glancing at me every minute or two. Internally, I was screaming *"Bitch, I know you're talking about me. I'm right here."* While on the outside I looked as cool as a cucumber.

Instead of coming up with a plan on what to tell them when they started asking questions, I sat dejectedly next to Sissily, more worried that she wasn't talking to me.

"Did I say I was sorry?" I whispered as low as I could before wobbling the chair and dragging it closer to her. "Because I am. Sorry, I mean."

Getting up, she pulled her seat away before plopping back on it with an annoyed huff.

I dragged mine next to her again with a loud scrape that cut off all the buzzing conversations in the office and brought all the eyes focused on us.

"We're good," I drawled at the gawkers. "Carry on with your gossiping and judgmental stares. We can wait."

"I see she's as insubordinate as I've been told," the clapper who'd applauded my fight with the Anger demon broke the silence, watching me with some glee I couldn't quite understand but could take a guess about.

"We are taught in this coven to always speak the truth." I locked eyes with my grandmother, daring her to say something. Icebergs had more warmth, or humanity, than the green orbs staring back at me. "If I misspoke, please feel free to correct me." My smile was so sweet it could've given her diabetes.

"I like her," said the second witch who'd accompanied my grandmother on the street where they found me bathed in blood with the concrete split from one side to the other like an erected barrier dividing the city. "She is full of fire." His eyes at least were sparkling with excitement.

Muttering and whispers started again throughout the large office.

"It sets a bad precedent..." the female grumbled, but Danika had reached her limit of silence while others talked. It was usually her who held court between these walls and the rest of us rushed to do whatever she commanded.

"Why does the goddess wish to test me so today," my

grandmother said in such a soft, conversational tone that no one should've heard her, yet you could hear a pin drop.

I swallowed thickly.

Old habits do die hard.

"Do you presume to tell me how to run my coven, Delores?" She did that thing with her head when she addressed the female where she cocked it slightly to the side, but it didn't look like a natural reaction to convey interest or curiosity in a person. It was more like a creepy bird of prey debating if it should eat you now or a little bit later. "Between these walls we refrain from lies and trickery. My granddaughter may be in need of polishing, but she is very young. You, on the other hand, should know better."

Instantly I sucked in my lips and bit on them so I didn't bark out a laugh. It was a trip to listen to Danika Byrne lecture someone about truths and lies. That was rich, coming from her deceitful ass. Something both Ace and Sissily must've agreed on because Ace grabbed my shoulder in a tight grip from where he stood behind our chairs, and Sissily sunk her nails into my thigh.

"Does this mean you're not angry with me anymore?" I breathed to my best friend.

She removed her hand from my leg.

Damn it.

"Apologies, High Priestess of the Gatekeeper coven." The gloater, now known as Delores, which suited her perfectly if you asked me, bowed slightly to my grandmother. Not necessarily a sign of respect but more of a "I was put on the spot' type of a show. "I meant no disrespect."

She totally meant it, and her clenched jaw only confirmed what all of us could see.

"That remains to be seen." Danika dismissed her with a

flick of her elegant hand, but kept her frozen with her icy glare. "I do, however, want to know who spoke so *highly* of my grandchild that it reached you all the way in Spain."

"And that was your mistake." The male witch grinned at Delores from ear to ear as he folded his arms across his chest. The cufflink blinking at me had the symbol of fire on it. No wonder he was so excited about my sass. Fire witches admired passion, regardless of what form it came in.

Ignoring him, Delores stayed in the staring match with my grandmother. At a couple of inches disadvantage, the Spanish witch had to tilt her head back to keep eye contact. Something Danika delighted in, I was sure of it.

"You know how it is." Delores giggled nervously, waving her hand to indicate the rest of us in the room. "People talk. How can I remember who has mentioned it in passing?"

"The same way you remembered what they said." Danika kept her expressionless face and watched the forced smile slip from the other witch's lips.

"I have requested to know more about her, if you must know." Dropping all pretenses, Delores finally found her spine. As much as I immediately disliked her, I wanted to return the favor and start clapping.

I did stay quiet, though, and tried to blend in with the crowd. The more Delores got Danika's attention, the better it was for me. Hopefully they'd start arguing and forget about my encounter with the demon. A girl could only hope.

"The whole community is talking about her and the way she nearly destroyed your precious coven. Did you think we would turn a blind eye at something like that?" With an indignant huff, she shook her head at Danika, ruffling her perfectly smooth red bob cut. "They can all pretend outrage at my audacity, but all of them are here for her. We want to know what is happening here."

"What is happening here?" Danika repeated, and a smile sharper than a blade tugged at her blood-red painted lips.

All the short hairs on my body perked up at attention when the air in the room was suddenly filled with electrical charge and the stench of ozone. My heart picked up speed and Sissily latched onto my arm, lifting me off the chair and pulling me with her toward the window on the far side of the office. Ace moved with us, keeping his body between the two of us and the rest of the people in the room. But I was laser focused on my grandmother.

Danika's hand lifted as if she wanted to cup the cheek of the other witch. Delores's eyes widened, and she took a step back in hopes to defend herself, but she was just a moment too late. Electricity discharged out from my grandmother's fingertips and penetrated the other female's skin. Her face twisted in agony, her mouth opening in a silent scream, but no sound came out. Slowly, Delores lifted off the ground and came at eye level with Danika who still looked like a statue with zero expression on her pretty face.

"High Priestess, I do believe she learned her lesson." The male witch gently placed a hand on my grandmother's forearm. When she didn't kill him on the spot, he leaned close to her ear and started whispering something none of us could hear.

The male was brave, I'd give him that much. I wouldn't go anywhere near Danika if I didn't have to on the best of days. Physically restraining her when she was pissed was suicide. A small spark of hope came to life inside me when Sissily and I turned to each other and shared one of our pointed looks. My best friend was back, although I was sure

I still had to pay for knocking her out and leaving her behind.

The rest of the witches, a dozen or so from all over the world judging by their clothing and looks, were plastered to the walls closest to them, hoping to stay as far away from the disaster unfolding in front of our eyes. Ace was the only one unconcerned about one person in particular. He stood with his legs shoulder width apart and glared at all of them, effectively preventing anyone from coming near us. His cell phone was also pressed to his ear, but I couldn't hear what he was saying or if he was saying anything at all.

Delores shrieked, and I watched horrified how blood trickled down her nose. It was a stark contrast over her blanched face which was what snapped me out of the stunned stupor I was in. One quick look at the male witch on the other side of Danika told me he was as lost as the rest of them over what to do. There was no doubt in my mind that my grandmother was about to kill an important member of the delegation. A quick look around showed that all of them were hoping that would happen, too.

A rock dropped in the pit of my stomach.

Like we were not all sinking in the proverbial creek. And all everyone was trying to do was protect me when I was the last person in need of their help. I was the monster still covered in blood which was drying and flaking with each move all over Danika's expensive rugs. Everyone that tried to hurt me so far was either dead or licking their wounds, hiding in some hole.

Murder in plain sight of one of our own was the last thing we needed.

Taking a deep breath to center myself, I reached deep inside me where the vortex of all the magic resided, ever restless, always ready at the smallest provocation to rush out and destroy something. Unlike other attempts when I'd tried to guide it, this time the bright light in my mind's eye teasingly jumped toward me like a playful child. Was it too much to hope that killing the demon paid the pound of blood it needed and now it'd play nice?

I had to trust that it would do the right thing.

"Release her." The voice that came out of my mouth was not my own.

I heard Sissily gasp, but she didn't let go of my arm. Instead, she tightened her hold, offering her support.

A collective gasp turned all eyes from the drama unfolding behind my grandmother's desk to me. Including Danika's. Her eyes were glowing with inner power, the emerald irises sparkling with suppressed wrath. I'd told her to release her toy, and she was not happy about it.

"I said release her." The echo of my voice made gooseflesh pimple my skin.

Disappointment stabbed me when Ace took a couple of steps to the side, adding space between us. Did he think I would hurt him?

"You forget who you are speaking to, Hazel," my grandmother snarled, showing any type of emotion for the first time. Her power intensified, and Delores screamed again, arching her back in midair.

"I'll accept my punishment for speaking out of turn, but first you must release her." Danika dangerously narrowed her eyes at me, and for whatever reason, it made me smile. "Or I will make you."

The foundations of the coven building started shaking as if an impending earthquake was about to strike. Thick books topped off the bookshelves around the office along with some tchotchkes she had sprinkled in various places.

The tremor made all the alcohol bottles on the bar in the corner jingle as they tapped against each other.

I really didn't want everyone to see roots and plants coming out of the floor. The street could've been explained, somehow. I hoped. But if I did it in the office in front of everyone, there was no explaining that. Whatever the case, I was running out of time. Delores began twitching, the fingers on the hand I could see spasming uncontrollably.

And Danika had a shit eating grin on her face that held no humor.

"That's enough." Throwing my hand in front of me, I sent as much power at my grandmother as I thought would be enough to force her to release the other witch. My magic had a different idea, though, so instead of the usual rope of power I was used to witnessing, a golden chain-like strand burst out of my palm. It lashed out at Danika, catching the side of her face as well as her shoulder, hip and arm. Everywhere my power touched it left a bright red welt of burnt skin. The black, skintight dress ripped as well, exposing her smooth skin underneath it.

Either the shock or the pain made her obey me, but Danika dropped her arm and rocked back on her heels. Grabbing hold of her desk was the only thing holding her upright, and my heart skipped a beat when her hair escaped the carefully positioned high ponytail.

Delores was gasping and coughing at my grandmother's feet, rubbing on her neck with a shaky hand.

I panted hard, as if I'd run a marathon, still shaking from the strength of the power. And from fear that I had scarred Danika for life. She was as conceited as me, I got that from her. She would never forgive me for marring her perfect appearance. With that in mind, I braced for retaliation.

"Next time," Danika spoke slowly, lifting her head and glaring first at everyone gathered in the office and ending it at a shrinking Delores. "When you decide to speak ill of my granddaughter, remember that it was her who saved your life."

"Holy shit, she planned it all," Sissily breathed for my ears only.

"Did she?" I muttered back, but I found Danika's gaze.

The small smile playing on her lips gave me a sinking feeling that what happened was not all that she planned.

"All of you, get out," my grandmother commanded, and all of us hurried to do just that, but my legs were cut at the knees. "Not you, Hazel."

Chapter Ten

"You had no right to agree to anything on my behalf," I repeated louder, angry as hell that Ace promised Danika I would return the next day to perform a spell for the delegation so they could see that the rumors were just that. Rumors. My magic was not destructive. Or dangerous to all.

"Do you really want to yell at us after you knocked us down and left us unconscious so you could play a hero?" Sissily chirped from the passenger seat.

"You of all people should back me up on this, girl. I'm not a monkey in a zoo." Annoyed, I slapped the seat and jerked my body backward on the leather in my version of an adult tantrum.

"I hate to break it to you, but you are in a zoo." Calmly fixing her ponytail and smoothing out stray strands, she sounded almost reasonable. "I mean, did you see them? They want things to change and not you, not Danika, nor anyone else is going to stop them. They stood there and wouldn't have moved a finger if you didn't help that bitch

Delores, either. All of them are willing to pay with blood if need be to get what they came for."

Ace hummed his agreement but said nothing otherwise. A muscle was jumping on one side of his jaw and his knuckles were white while he gripped the steering wheel. We bounced on the uneven road toward pack lands a half hour after Danika dismissed all of us and locked herself with the male witch in her office. Poor Delores bolted like the wind out of the coven. None of us blamed her.

"That has nothing to do with me." I stubbornly continued to argue even though I knew she was right. If I pretended to ignore it, it would go away.

Right.

"On the contrary, it has everything to do with you." My best friend took a deep breath and scrubbed a hand over her face tiredly. "I wish River was awake. He would know what to do, I'm sure of it."

Ace stiffened but said nothing.

"You know saying contrary makes you sound like an old broad, right?"

"The same way changing the subject makes you an ass?" she asked sweetly. "Why, yes. Yes, I know."

"I learned how to control the power for the most part, and when I do use it, any mishap doesn't count against me since I'm usually trying to kill whoever is coming after us." Twisting my fingers in my lap, I stared straight through the windshield at the darkness broken by the headlights of the SUV. Trees loomed on both sides as we passed, their branches occasionally slapping the sides of the vehicle. "Casting a spell is a different story. All sorts of things can go wrong."

"We can practice." Unease crept up on her features as

well, but she nodded once, firmly convincing herself more than me. "I'll help you."

"We should maybe do it out here somewhere." Limply flopping a hand at the window, I locked eyes with Ace in the rearview mirror. "The only things that can get hurt here if something goes wrong are the trees."

Not that I wanted to go in the middle of the woods at night to practice spells. I wanted to go to bed, curl up under the covers, and forget the day all together. After I showered and washed the dry blood and gore off me, of course. On that note, I gingerly took a hardened lump of crusted hair between my two fingers and tried unsuccessfully to move it away from my face. It was a no go. The thing was like a piece of plaster stuck to the side of my face.

"First we will go and get back up. Report to Alex and see if any new information has come about the situation." Ace sounded like the words were forced out of his lips. Smudges were visible under his eyes too, so I decided not to argue with him. "Then we can decide if you can practice in the woods."

"Aye, aye, captain." My two-finger salute didn't even make Ace crack a smile.

Guilt stabbed me for giving him a hard time while he had his own problems to deal with. It couldn't be easy for someone with such strong instincts and personality to brush off an almost forced shift and being knocked out by my magic straight afterward.

"Sorry, Ace." Reaching in front of me, I squeezed his shoulder. "I don't mean to be an ass. I'm just rattled, and as you know by now, this is how I deal with crap."

"I know." The growl in his tone had softened a little. "I'm on the edge too. That's why I think it's safer for everyone to get to the Alpha first. We can make a game plan later."

"Hopefully River is awake, as well," Sissily murmured softly almost to herself, but when she glanced back at me, she squared her shoulders. "Don't ask me why, but I have this gut feeling that he is the solution to all our problems."

"I did tell you in confidence that he can use the angel magic to destroy anyone, but he won't do it or he will be in bigger danger than me."

The SUV screeched to a stop so suddenly I was catapulted between the two front seats, my head aiming straight for the large screen on the dashboard. Sissily squealed and hugged the windshield first with a loud crack, and I followed a second behind her. Both of us crumpled in a lump with a tangle of limbs while the gear stick lodged itself between my boobs.

"Are we under attack?" Sissily and I said at the same time, grunting and shoving at each other to untangle ourselves.

Tucking her elbow under my chest, Sissily heaved me up and without too much effort propelled me back in the seat. Ears ringing from hitting my forehead on the console, I rubbed between my eyebrows while turning around wildly to check if I could spot our attackers in the darkness. Sissily was ready too, with one leg tucked under her on the seat, she had the door open and lightning was forking from her fingertips toward the sky.

"You want to tell me, Blackman, the same male that you two brought on our land, has angel magic that can destroy my entire pack and none of you found it necessary to inform me?"

"Did you miss the seven-foot span of pigeon wings he sprouted when we were attacked by the Mazzikin?" I spoke slowly in case he hit his head too. "Or when we dragged him unconscious back from Hell and had to use chairs next to the bed to spread them up so they don't break?"

"If you hit those brakes and made me headbutt that windshield for this, Ace, I swear to Hecate I'm going to load you up with lightning until you pop like a kernel of popcorn," Sissily snarled like a feral raccoon, and I had to bite my lip when I looked at her so I didn't bark out a laugh. A lump the size of a goose egg was forming on the right side of her forehead and was rapidly growing as I watched. "And if you make another sound, Hazel, you will suffer the same fate even if it kills me." She slammed the door closed, but the tips of her fingers were crackling.

That's when I noticed that I was making soft choking sounds. Mimicking a zipping motion in front of my lips, I swallowed the laughter bubbling in my chest. She wasn't joking at all, her scowl darkening with each breath.

"He has witch magic." Ace sounded defensive, as if that explained everything, while eyeing Sissily warily. "I thought the wings were an unfortunate side effect of his mongrel bloodline."

"I'd dare you to say that to his face," I drawled and rubbed between my breasts where I had no doubt I was already sporting a bruise.

"I thought you didn't like him." The shifter dared to go there.

"I don't, but right now I don't like you much either." Pressing on my eyes to relieve the pressure headache that started developing, I promised myself I would stay calm. "River is not going to hurt anyone in your pack. He even fought to protect you guys if you don't remember. Besides, Alex knows everything and he trusted him among his family. Do you think your Alpha needed your permission for any of it? Just start the car and get us to the house. I need a shower more than I need to strangle you."

"I can't do what's expected of me if I'm not given all the information," Ace grumbled but started up the car and we were on our way again.

"You can put some ice on it when we get to the house." Leaning forward, I stuck my head in my friend's space. "It doesn't even look that bad."

"Really?" Dust could've puffed out between her lips from the flatness of her tone.

"Actually, it does look bad." Taking her chin in my hand, I turned her face to the side to see better. The dashboard lights cast strange shadows across her face, but the lump was clear as day. "It looks like you are growing a chesticle on your forehead. It has a nipple, too." I prodded at the lump gently, and she slapped my finger with a glare.

"The limit of how much crazy I can tolerate from you in one day is reached, woman." She tried to avoid my hand while she spoke, but I grabbed the back of her neck to hold her still. "Would you stop? Grow up!"

Ignoring her protests, I focused on the churning magic inside me thumping down the always present fear that I might hurt someone with it. I might not know anything about the Fae but the myths couldn't be that far-fetched. They could even bring back the dead if they so wished it. It meant their magic could heal too. I just had to believe that it would do my will. With that firmly in mind, I allowed a trickle to go into Sissily, begging it to help her and promising to trust it more if it didn't hurt my friend.

Sissily stiffened but didn't push me away. She just latched onto my arm like her life depended on it, which I supposed it did. My breath hitched when the lump lit up like a bulb, my power flickering through it for a long moment. It illuminated her face and mine, but it dissipated too fast for me to examine it closely. As it faded, it smoothed out her forehead but lingered longer than I was comfortable with, curiously testing Sissily's magic before returning through my fingertips where it belonged.

Stunned, we watched each other with wide eyes until Ace cleared his throat. Like it or not, he had a front seat to our lives now.

"That was weird," he grumbled, watching the road with one eye and us with the other.

"You say that like it's a bad thing." The rest of whatever was going to come out of my mouth was forgotten when we passed the gates and the large house came into view.

It felt like I'd been gone for months. And strangely enough, it felt more like home than Danika's house ever had. The tightness of my shoulders eased; the pressure headache was gone, and I felt like I could take a full breath for the first time in days. A smile stretched my lips when I saw Jack yanking the door open and running down the few steps toward the car, his hair that'd grown too long flopping over one eye.

"Troublemaker!" Opening the door while Ace was still rolling to a stop, I jumped out and snatched the rascal in my arms as soon as he reached me. "I'll get you dirty and your mother will kill me."

"Hazel!" Jack squealed and squeezed around me with arms and legs like a boa constrictor. "No, she won't." He laughed and giggled when I poked his ribs and started tickling him and then growled an involuntary warning, his wolf wanting to play too. "I have great news to tell you, and she is too happy to worry about laundry tonight."

"Jack the ripper." Sissily joined us, stealing a quick kiss to Jack's head before he could dodge her.

"I'm not a ripper. I'm a wolf," he argued, his irises flashing to confirm his statement.

"Hmmm, could've fooled me, kid. You look like a ripper." She looked at him sideways and nodded to herself.

"Hey, hey." Holding him tighter when he tried to wiggle out of my arms to probably shift and bite Sissily's ankles, I struggled to get his attention. "You were going to tell me great news, remember?"

"Oh, yeah," he breathed, forgetting all about Sissily's teasing. She rolled her eyes. "Guess what, Hazel? Guess what?"

"Ummmm...I have no idea, Jack. Please tell me." Smiling at his eagerness, I nearly tripped on flat ground when he shared his great news.

"River is awake."

Chapter Eleven

"I was first to tell Hazel the great news," Jack announced to everyone mingling in the foyer the moment my feet carried both of us inside the large home his parents built.

Sissily, who followed right behind me, snickered softly at the kid, who preened in my arms like he had conquered the world. It was difficult not to smile around Jack. He'd decided Sissily and I were his people, so he hung out with us every chance he got, going as far as shifting and curling up at my feet overnight as his wolf.

"They're here?" Amber popped her head out of Alex's office down the hall like she'd been sitting there with the door open, waiting.

"I found them," Jack told her somberly, and I grinned from ear to ear, shaking my head.

Amber waved us in her direction and disappeared inside, so I hurried my steps to see what the urgency was. But before I could enter the office, both she and Alex walked out, brushing past me to start deeper into the house and down the long hallway.

"You're here. Good," Alex grumbled, not even looking at me. "Follow me."

"Can it wait so I can wash the demon off me?" I muttered grudgingly.

"No," the Alpha growled, which effectively killed all other comments and questions I had.

"She used to smell so nice all the time." Jack had no qualms about speaking his mind regardless of whether his father was angry. I wished I was as brave as the kid. "She's always stinky now." Scrunching up his little nose, he bared his teeth at me.

"Don't hold back, Jack. Tell me how you really feel." I jostled the little rascal, and he giggled evilly at me.

All the humor evaporated when Alex opened the back door and we all trickled after him outside. He didn't stop, just continued walking across the large expanse of the back yard, his long legs eating up the space so fast the rest of us were jogging to catch up to him. Skipping cardio was starting to show, and I tucked Jack behind me so he could hang like a monkey on my back. The pup was skinny as a rail but weighed a ton.

Sissily caught up with me, and we looked at each other. Whatever was going on, it had pissed Alex off to no end, and I secretly hoped it had nothing to do with River. The pigeon annoyed me—through no fault of his own for the most part—but I didn't want him hurt or hated. If Sissily and I had to suffer coven politics and other bullshit, he needed to take his fair share of misery, as well.

We were halfway across the large expense of property when a massive wolf loped toward us, followed by two smaller ones. On pack lands it could've been any shifter, but the moment I locked eyes with the one coming at us, I knew it was Ace. He finally caught up with us after parking the

SUV and whatever else he did. The smaller wolves bracketed their Alpha, one on each side, but Ace came in the middle of Sissily and me, shouldering a space between us when we didn't move fast enough for his liking. Sinking my fingers in his fur, I tugged harshly, making him snarl at me, but I had to tell him somehow to stop being a jerk.

"I didn't know this was here," Sissily whispered for my ears only, but Amber heard her and quickly gave her a glance over the shoulder.

It was a shed.

There were no other ways to describe the wooden structure roughly put together like someone came up with the idea and they used whatever material was handy to hold it up. Different colored planks and tiles gave it a cute, rustic feel until I focused better on the darker patches on the walls. The more I looked at them, the more they resembled blood stains than dark colored wooden planks.

Alex yanked the door open and held it as he waved all of us to get in. Amber zoomed inside along with the two smaller wolves so I didn't second guess it either. Hiking Jack higher on my back, I walked in with Ace and Sissily hot on my heels.

And froze on the spot a few steps inside the door.

"I don't know who can listen to our conversation in the house." Alex spoke from behind me as he closed the door.

"I don't mean to be a negative Nancy but you think this is more secure?" Circling the structure with my finger, I kept throwing glances at the witch Danika was interrogating who was now tied to a chair on Pack lands.

"It's warded to silence, for..." Alex's mismatched eyes softened slightly when he looked at his son perched on my back. "Well, for obvious reasons. Your grandmother did the warding herself on my request."

"That's my concern, more than anything else," I told him truthfully.

"Danika is the least of our problems."

Rounding the bunch of us clustered near the door, Alex walked up to the witch and slapped him a few times to wake him up. The wolves positioned themselves at the corners of the space, ready to pounce at a second's notice. With ears pinned to the back of their skulls, their upper lip was pulled back, exposing long sharp teeth. In a blink of an eye, Amber shifted too, her red wolf perching right in front of the chair just in time for the witch to see her and scream as loud as a banshee.

Alex backhanded him, cutting off the shriek.

"I told you everything I know." The male's high-pitched tone sounded nasal, probably from the broken nose that sat crooked on his face.

"Not everything." The gravelly voice coming from deep within the Alpha's chest was a thing of nightmares.

"The High Priestess..." the witch started fearfully, shrinking into the metal chair as much as he could, and I frowned at him.

What other things has Danika stirred up now?

"Your High Priestess can't help you now," Alex told him, planting his boot on the chair between the male's legs and leaning on his bent knee. "Nobody knows where you are, as I told you, and unless you like it here and don't want to leave, I'd start talking."

Jostling Jack who was still clinging to my back, I looked back to check on the kid, expecting to see him worried or scared. I should've known better because Jack was his father's son. He glared at the witch, and I fully expected him to jump down and slap the male himself.

"I told you they promised me a place on the council,"

the male stuttered, craning his head back to stay as far away from Alex as possible. "All I had to do was pour the potion they gave me into all the bottles of alcohol sitting on the bar in the High Priestess's office. That's it."

Bile rose inside me at the reminder of how sick I felt from drinking that whisky. It was strange to get that bad from half a bottle since I was not a lightweight drinker, but I never gave it too much thought. Hearing that it was spiked with an unknown potion made new acid swirl in my belly.

"What type of a potion?" My question came out as a croak.

The witch blinked and tilted sideways to try and see me, blanching at the sight of me when he finally realized he, the wolves, and the Alpha were not alone.

"More importantly, who gave you the potion?" Alex looked pointedly at me over his shoulder.

"I don't know what the potion does, I never asked," the male rushed to say only to get backhanded again.

"Who. Gave. You. The. Potion?" Alex said slowly, and the red wolf leaned forward with a fear-inducing growl.

"The Magistrates," the male squealed, jerking back in his chair. "I don't know her name, or his. There were two of them. Two," he repeated and pissed himself, the stench of urine spreading around the shed within seconds.

"Aww," Jack gagged quietly and started wiggling in my grip, so I let him slide down.

My mind was reeling. I could guess who the female was without a problem, but the male? I lost my train of thought when I saw that Jack shifted too and jumped on the witch's legs to pee on his lap. The pup must've thought the witch was marking a territory so he rushed to show him that all this land was his. My lips twitched and I heard Sissily cough softly to cover a snort.

"Did she have red hair?" My best friend folded her arms across her chest and looked down her nose at the male. "Sharp, bob cut?"

"Th...Ya...Yes." the witch stuttered.

We looked at each other.

"You two know who this person is?" There was a note of pride in the Alpha's tone, and my chest puffed up slightly.

"She showed her true colors earlier after they saw me killing the Anger demon downtown." I answered, and the red wolf turned her head to look me up and down as a reminder that I kept my promise to her and came back alive.

Warmth spread through my chest and I hoped she could see how much I appreciated her in my gaze.

"What of the male?" I asked just as Alex swatted the pup off the male's legs. "What did he look like?"

"I don't rem..." he started, but his words were cut off when Alex moved lightning fast, grabbed him by the throat, and lifted him up, chair and all. Coughing and sputtering, the witch slowly started turning purple, his feet kicking weakly in the air.

"Umm, he needs air," Sissily chirped conversationally, and I snickered.

I mean, it was a shitty time to laugh but sometimes her Captain Obvious moments did that to me. I could be dead, and if she said something similar, I'd come back just to chortle.

Alex dropped the male with a loud smack of the chair legs on the wooden planks that served as floor. The witch gasped and coughed, drooling all over himself.

"Do you remember now?" Sissily leaned forward, placing her hands on her thighs. "As you noticed by now, this here is no longer coven business. Different rules apply on Pack lands. We can't help you unless you give us the information we need."

"I did not see him," the male rasped, and his eyes widened comically when Alex took a step toward him. "He had a mask," he shrieked. "A face covering. To hide himself. A mask. To cover his face."

"You two broke him," I told them. "He's a blubbering fool now."

"He had a water drop on his cufflink." Shaking uncontrollably, the witch repeated the same thing three times before falling silent.

"Now tell me who else was there," Alex snarled so viciously that even I took a step back.

It was time to see why the Alpha was spitting mad and ordered all of us here.

Jack, who was silently sitting next to his mother, growled adorably at the witch.

"No…" Causing the chair to rattle from the force of his tremors, the male sagged in the restraints dejectedly. "Why do I care anyway? They are going to kill me even if you don't."

"Who. Was. There?"

"Whoever made you do this signed your death sentence. Why are you protecting them?" I genuinely wanted to know.

"We don't see them coming to your help, and they know we captured you," Sissily pointed out, which actually made sense. The delegation knew we had a culprit in custody for sneaking around the coven.

"Wait." I turned to Alex. "Why is he here and not in the coven? Danika doesn't usually give away her toys."

"She asked me to bring him here after someone tried to

kill him ten minutes after the delegation arrived," he told me with an intense look on his face.

It made sense why he was upset and told Ace not to let me out of his sight. A loud slap made us both jerk from the sudden sound just to see Sissily rub her hand on her jeans.

"That hurt." She scrubbed her hand harder with a grimace twisting her features. "Answer the question. Who else?"

"A wolf," the witch said to the floor, his voice barely audible. "There was a brown wolf with them but he or she never shifted so I don't know what they look like."

Cold sweat drenched me. All brown or gray wolves plus the red one belonged to Alex's pack. Could it be that that bitch had sold me to Hell just to get me out of the way? Anger bubbled up inside me and the same moment nausea made the shed swim in front of my eyes. Stumbling to the side, I would've fallen if Sissily hadn't grabbed me by the arm.

Alex stood frozen, waves of fury coming off of him in droves. Even Amber was growling deep in her throat followed by the rest of the shifters with us. They took any type of betrayal personally, regardless if it was for a good reason. The Alpha wouldn't rest until they were brought to justice by pack law. He would fight them to death.

"See if you can find who it was." Alex turned to Ace who hadn't moved since he took up his position.

Frowning, I watched the wolf wait at the door until Sissily opened it before he bolted like an arrow as soon as he had a free exit. Confused as hell, I had to know what was going on, despite the fact that I was wary of saying anything to Alex when he was that pissed.

"How would he know who the wolf was? You think they'll just out themselves if Ace asks?"

"Apart from us here in this room none of my pack has been around a witch. If they have, we can smell the magic on them." Alex looked at me, and my heart skipped a beat when his mismatched eyes flashed with rage. "If they're here. He will find them."

Shocked, I just watched him, my mouth opening into a silent O. Sissily was just as shocked, her eyebrows blending in with her hairline. That was until Jack shifted back to a boy—buck naked with his lingonberries wiggling around.

"I told you that you stink now, Hazel." He looked up at me, grinning from ear to ear.

Just what every woman wanted to hear.

"Thanks, buddy," I drawled, and Sissily—the jerk—snickered.

Chapter Twelve

Lesson 18: *When you think things can't get any worse, the Fates prove you wrong.*

Surprisingly I felt calm in the grand scheme of things. Until we did some testing, no one could guess what the potion I ingested could do. While Ace searched for the brown wolf who was an accomplice to Delores and the masked male, we had to wait. And I was in desperate need of a shower where I spent a good forty-five minutes at least. It could've been more.

All cleaned up, and according to Jack the rascal, dressed in less stinky clothing, I smoothed my blouse and checked my appearance once more before raising my fist and rapping my knuckles on the door.

"Come in."

River's voice came out raspy from unuse, yet it still made my belly flip-flop. Something I would never admit to him or anyone else. I was a commitment-phobe when my life was uneventful. It would be the dumbest thing to entangle myself with someone like the pigeon now when everything around me was shitstorm in a handbasket.

"I heard you were done with your beauty sleep," I told River as I entered, busying myself with closing the door so I didn't gawk at him.

He didn't have to be shirtless on the bed. Had he never heard of a t-shirt?

"Hazel." Hearing my name pebbled my skin with goosebumps. "It's good to see that you are well. Amber told me, but it's better to confirm with my own eyes."

"Ditto, buddy." And I wanted to slap myself. Who even said that? An idiot like me probably, that was who.

Unable to avoid looking at him, I locked my gaze on his and forced it to stay there. If it slipped a few times greedily down his bare torso, I pretended not to notice. It was his fault for not wearing a shirt after all, not mine. He kept staring at me without a word.

"You gave us a scare." It was acceptable to talk about our trip to Hell without getting too personal. "Not gonna lie to you, there were a couple of times where I didn't think any of us were making it out alive."

"My apologies, Hazel." Lowering the chocolate irises, he fisted a hand on top of the covers. "I failed you. I failed both of you."

"We are still talking about my impulsive decision to go to Hell, right?" When he looked at me blankly, I shrugged. "Just checking. Because if anyone should be sorry about that disaster, it should be me."

And because River always unsettled me to a point where I couldn't think straight, I lowered my butt on the bed next to his leg.

"We could've prepared better, yes, but even then we couldn't have known that they would be expecting us." With a shake of his head that made his hair flop over his forehead, he glared at his still clenched fist. "Who had the time to inform them when we didn't know that day that we would be entering the portal."

"That's actually a good question," I conceded before I had to backtrack. "Wait, you are guessing they knew we were coming, or you're sure?"

"They knew." The snarl in his voice told me he knew something I didn't.

"I'll share what you've missed, if you share, too." Remembering that it wasn't just us two involved in the mess, I attempted to stand up and call Sissily to join us. "Let me get…"

"Stay." He had my hand in his, and I barely saw him move. "We can call the others later. If you don't mind, I would like to have a talk with just you."

I could bet my magic that River could hear my heart thumping so hard because it was vibrating the fabric of my blouse. The way I was bent, half up and off the bed, placed us closer than necessary with our faces. I could see the flakes in his irises disappear and reappear as his pupils dilated and retracted. There was also a strand of hair covering his eyebrow that I wanted to reach out and smooth away.

Panic that I might just do that gripped me and lodged itself like a fist in my throat.

"I think I was poisoned in the last twenty-four hours." I blurted out the first thing that came to mind which was sure to kill any ideas of petting hair or kissing. Yeah, because kissing was out of the question.

Indefinitely.

"Poisoned?" His face transformed from calm and remorseful to focused and sharp. "Surely someone did something to reverse it. There must be an antidote regardless of what kind of poison it is." He was already pulling on my eyelids, turning my face this way and that between his palms. "Did they?" When I didn't answer fast enough for his liking, he shook me like a rag doll. "Hazel, focus! Did they give you an antidote?"

I could've sworn I heard him mumble to himself, "I knew something was off when you were all nice."

"Hey!" Slapping his grabby hands away, I scowled at him. "My eyelids are attached to my face. Well, they used to be. If you ripped them off, I'll pluck your feathers one by one, River Blackman."

"Maybe the poison was not deadly." Tilting his head to the side, he studied me intently. "You seem like yourself now. I was a little worried when you came in, but you're you now."

"Very funny." Scooting out of reach on the bed, I folded my hands in my lap. "You go first."

"They had an angel trap ready and knew exactly what to do to try and steal my grace." Dark thoughts clouded his face. "If I was full angel, they would've succeeded. Luckily, my mixed heritage saved my life."

"Grace, as in your soul?" I had to confirm it because that would've been the only thing that made sense.

"Not really, but it's the closest thing to an explanation."

"Such a demon thing to do." Annoyed on his behalf, I stared at my hands. "What, they gonna mount it on the wall to show off?"

"They would absorb it if they managed to steal it." My horrified expression had him explaining more. "The grace of an angel would give anyone who absorbs it the power to walk undetected through any portal in any realm. It amplifies their power, too."

He waited, watching me absorb that information. My

mind was doing loops, bouncing off one ramification to another until it screeched to a stop and my eyes widened.

"What are the chances that they have an angel trap just sitting in Hell for 'in case' scenarios? We know that bitch sold us out when the pack was attacked by Mazzikin, but she couldn't have known you would be coming with me. She wanted me gone, not you."

"How many angels have you met or seen in your lifetime?" he countered, not answering my questions but allowing me to find my own conclusion.

"Sonofabitch." I jumped on my feet and started pacing at the foot of the bed. "How?" Pausing in front of him so he could see my perplexed expression, I waved with both hands at myself. "I didn't know I would go there with you tagging along an hour before we headed in the direction of the Hall of Fame. How can they be tipped?"

River blinked at me, his face not betraying anything.

"None of this makes sense," I told him harshly like it was his fault I couldn't figure out what was going on.

"We can circle back to that." He brushed it off like it was nothing. "Tell me about this poison."

"First tell me they didn't steal your soul." Saying that made my heart thump hard first in my stomach then bounce off the roof of my mouth.

"My grace, and no. They didn't steal it." Rubbing a fist between his pecs as if remembering a phantom pain, he lowered his hand when he saw me watching. "I had to be conscious for them to extract it. Having fire as my element from my witch ancestors helped me force myself in a suspended state. I literally overheated my body, causing it to switch itself off until it cooled down."

"Sissily and I thought they hurt you somehow."

"In a way they did." He clenched his jaw, and I thought it was time to change the subject.

"There is a delegation visiting the coven." Continuing my pacing, I waved with my hands as I spoke. "Danika didn't want me anywhere near them and tried to hide me. I was on my way to get out of dodge when an Anger demon attacked a full street of people, the majority of them humans." Remembering the day just got me more upset. "Before you ask, I was in the coven building because I wanted to tell Danika I want to start taking cases. Before I entered, I found a male who firstly was shocked that I was there in the middle of the day, and secondly that it was me who he bumped into. He attacked and I knocked his lights. What I didn't know at the time was that he spiked all the drinks in Danika's office with an unknown potion."

Closing my eyes, I took a deep breath and centered myself before continuing. Repeating the whole thing, even in Reader's Digest form made me want to cry. Thankfully, River stayed silent, giving me my time.

"I drank half a bottle of whisky before Ace took it from me." A look passed over his face, but it was so fast I didn't fully catch it. "It made me sick, but I didn't think anything of it until I returned here and Alex made the male confess everything. Danika tried unsuccessfully then dropped the witch on the Alpha after someone tried to kill him while in coven custody." Sucking in a deep breath, I lifted both hands in surrender. "And here we are. I'm still nauseous as hell but at least I'm not dead, yet. Unlike the wolf when Alex finds him or her. They were present with the two witches when they recruited the male to poison the drinks."

"And we know who they are?" River threw the covers to the side and stood up.

I nearly swallowed my tongue seeing him in boxers and nothing else.

"Hmm?" Dragging my eyes up and away from his boxers, I felt my cheeks heat up seeing him smirk at me. "What was the question?"

"Do we know who those witches are?" He indulged me without making fun of me.

Subtly, I checked if I was drooling, and luckily, I wasn't.

"Delores and a masked male." With a shrug I turned my back on him so he could dress.

"Delores the High Priestess from Spain?"

"You know her?" I turned to frown at him, abandoning the idea of giving him privacy.

"Power hungry," was all he said.

"It seems everyone is these days." My muttering earned me a chuckle.

"But not you, Hazel Byrne." He walked up to me and pinched my chin between a thumb and a crooked forefinger.

"Can you put a shirt on?" I mumbled as I forced myself to not stare at his mouth. "You're very distracting."

A crooked smile curved his lips and for a second there I thought he was going to kiss me. "You are not power hungry at all," he whispered.

"I'm just happy I have any magic at all and I'm no longer a dud." For whatever reason, I answered him truthfully.

"That's why you deserve it all."

But I stopped paying attention to anything else he said because that was when it hit me.

"Ah, shit!" In frustration, I started kicking and muttering curses, pushing River a few steps away from me. "Shit. Shit, shit!"

"What is it?" River grabbed my arm to stop me from having my tantrum. "Speak, female!"

"It's not poison, River." A string of very unflattering sentences followed that statement that would've made Danika have an aneurism if she heard me.

"How do you know?" he turned motionless watching my every twitch of a muscle like the predator that he was.

"Because I can't lie," I shrieked my frustration to the ceiling. "It's a fucking truth serum."

Chapter Thirteen

Alex jumped to his feet when I barreled into his office like a Tasmanian devil with River hot on my heels. Whoever the other shifter was growled his displeasure, but one look from his Alpha silenced him immediately. As soon as he was dismissed and the door closed behind him, I rushed to the desk and slapped both my hands on it.

"It's a truth serum."

"Okay." The mismatched gaze of the Alpha jumped from me to River then back. "What is a truth serum?"

"The potion they made the male pour in the liquor was a truth serum not poison." Sucking in a huge breath, I held it for a second before expelling it in a huff. "Well, it could still be poison but it is a truth serum as well."

"They want to unearth what we know." Alex lowered himself slowly in the leather chair, but he was still holding the desk with a tight grip.

"We need to call Danika." I was already reaching for my back pocket to do just that. "As much as she deserves to get choked on a truth serum, if she spills family secrets, they will tear the Gatekeeper's coven to shreds and the two of us along with it."

"No one is going to touch you, Hazel." Alex dismissed my worry with a flick of his wrist. "Least of all any witch, I don't care how powerful they are. Not under my watch."

"I am a witch," I pointed out unnecessarily.

"You are." The Alpha was cut off by the door being open without a knock.

"She's special." Sissily waltzed in with a flair of a tornado and finished his sentence. "Good to see you up and about River."

"Have you heard of knocking?" I had to throw in a jab because she knew I hated that word 'special' and she used it on purpose.

"She's channeling her inner Hazel." River chuckled when I glared at him.

"You're not helping." Pinching the bridge of my nose, I took a couple of breaths. "We need to warn Danika so she doesn't go around sharing demonic heritage with the rest of the witch community."

"What did I miss?" Sissily perched on the arm of the chair Amber usually used in the office.

"The potion had a truth serum in it," I grumbled like a petulant child, and I tossed my cell phone on the desk with a clattering bounce after dialing a few times and hanging up when the voicemail was connected. "She's not picking up."

"Let me try." Sissily pulled her cell and tapped one foot while she waited, looking up at the ceiling instead of the rest of us. She tried once more before giving up with a shake of her head.

"I will send someone to bring her a message." Alex pulled out a piece of paper with the logo of Amber's café and started scribbling on it.

Despite the situation, a smile tugged at my lips at how the Alpha and his mate functioned as a couple. The gruff scary Alpha was putty in the hands of the female and he worshipped the ground she walked on. Instead of envy, warmth spread through me at their love. Another reminder that I had to get rid of the damn truth serum because I couldn't even lie to myself anymore.

"We could just go there." Sissily suggested tentatively while scratching her nails over the denim of her jeans. "Hazel has to perform a spell anyway. We can just go and get it over with while making sure Danika is aware she will be spilling the beans if she drank any of her liquor."

Alex stopped writing and raised his head to watch our stare off.

"Easy for you to say." I huffed, annoyed. "You're not the monkey."

"You are not the monkey." Upset, she stood up to scowl at me. "What is the matter with you, woman? You have enough power to turn them to ashes if they piss you off without breaking a sweat. You're scared of a bunch of old bats?"

"I'm not scared of them." Forgetting about the truth serum, I kept talking. "I'm afraid of myself." And I clamped my mouth shut.

River, who stood close to me, reached for my shoulder and gave it a quick squeeze, wisely retracting it quickly before I could bite his hand off. Uninvited physical contact was not in my repertoire, and I could deal with only so much of it per day.

"You won't be going alone." Alex leaned back in his chair, the note he was scribbling forgotten. "I will be coming with you."

"I've done enough damage to you and your pack

already." Was I really considering doing the spell that day? "I should deal with this alone."

"You have done nothing but seek shelter here as you should've." A thunder rolled in his expression, and his shoulders bunched up with it. "They chose to involve my wolves in their schemes. They chose to attack me and mine on clearly, and legally, marked territory. You can't take credit for that."

"So, I'll walk among monsters but I'll be okay because I'll carry a big stick, huh?" Scrubbing a hand over my face tiredly, I conceded. "Doesn't it show weakness to show up to perform a measly spell with a full entourage?"

A small, evil smile spread across Alex's face that sent chills down my spine.

"That depends on the entourage." He chuckled menacingly.

"The size of the stick is very important." River joined him in some male solidarity with all the big dick energy the two of them were throwing around.

Sissily giggled, giddily slapping her hands and rubbing them together. "This is going to be fun."

"For whom?" I drawled, but she ignored me. "Do we even have an idea on what spell I should do or am I winging it?"

"Hmm." Tapping a finger on her lips, my best friend looked me up and down through a narrowed gaze. "Your biggest strength is ancestral magic which is something we need to cover up. I wonder if it will work..."

"We are screwed. Sissily has no idea what she's talking about," I announced to the room to calm my nerves.

"As I was saying." She gave me a pointed glower. "You can perform a summoning spell where you invite the moon magic to assist you in making a seed grow."

"You are out of your ever-loving mind, Sissily Stormblood." My hand slicing through the air announced the reached limit of my patience. "There will be no Fae magic anywhere near that delegation."

"It could be a bad idea," Alex muttered more to himself than us but didn't sound convinced.

"Didn't you say they saw you in the middle of the street kneeling on the asphalt with roots ten feet up in the air growing in downtown Cleveland?" Sissily was not deterred one bit by my anger.

"So, you did listen to me although you pretended to ignore me and refused to speak." My finger stabbed the air accusingly in her direction.

"Of course I listened." My best friend snorted like I'd told her the dumbest thing under the sun. "I was pissed, not deaf."

"You didn't mention anything about roots when you told me what happened," River grumbled from where he stood just to the side of me. He had a shirt on, thank the goddess.

"You are worried more about growing roots than the Anger demon?"

"Pfft." The pigeon smirked and I wanted to slap it off his handsome face. "You could handle an Anger demon before you unlocked your magic, Hazel." That stupid smile grew on his mug and formed a small dimple on his left cheek. "Only a fool will underestimate you."

"Flattery won't get you anywhere with this one," Sissily mumbled while circling her hand my way.

"Actually, let the male speak." I waved her off. "Flattery will get him many places."

"Dear Hecate, I forgot about the truth serum. We will be

back after we come up with a spell. Bye." Jumping off the arm of the chair, she grabbed me by the hand and started yanking me toward the door. "Abort mission. Abort mission."

"You sound dumb." Snickering at her behavior, I allowed her to drag me out of the office. "Abort mission. What the fuck is that?"

Slamming the door shut behind us, she leaned on the wood and pressed my ear on it, too. "Listen." She whispered with a finger pressed to her lips. Our noses were so close I had to cross my eyes to look at her sign for silence.

I heard Alex say something too low for us to make out the words but there was no mistaking River's voice.

"I wish," River answered to whatever the Alpha commented.

Both of them laughed.

I frowned.

"You told Blackman flattery will get him places." Her eyebrows crawled up her forehead as she straightened up in front of me.

"Do we know how long truth serums have effect?" My groan sounded pained.

"No, but I can keep you from making a fool out of yourself until then." Threading her arm through mine, she tugged me down the hallway which was thankfully empty. "I think."

"Or die trying." My grumbling made her snicker.

"We'll be fine." She blew out a heavy sigh. "We're always fine, aren't we? Just need to get through this one hurdle and we're good."

"Yeah." Sagging on her elbow so she could carry most of my weight, I bumped her shoulder. "All we need to do is keep me away from professing my never-ending lust for

Blackman and blabbing out every damming thing about my ancestry to the delegation. Easy peasy."

"Lemon squeezy," Sissily added, and we both laughed as we sauntered toward my room.

I hoped we would not be crying by the time this was over.

Chapter Fourteen

"You need to hold still with your arms up. Like this," Sissily lectured, and I glared at her while she stretched toward the ceiling with her face tipped up and her spine straight.

"You look ridiculous, just so you know." With a grumble under my breath, I rolled my sore shoulders. "Why do you assume I didn't hear you the first ten times?"

"Because you look like a raccoon trying to look big and scare me instead of attempting to summon moon magic," she droned in a flat tone.

We agreed that her idea of making a seed grow was the best we could do to cover up the disaster with the roots when I fought the Anger demon. She convinced me that the spell was easy to remember and even easier to do. Little ones do it for fun around the sabbaths, she taunted me.

"Little ones, my ass. Who even forces seeds to grow?" Shaking off my hands to the sides, I prepared myself for one more try of summoning the moon to aid me. In the middle of the day, mind you. "You bury that shit in the ground and you wait. Witches should learn patience."

"And you should learn to zip the trap and follow directions." Her eyebrows arched up like some judgmental, negative Nancy.

"I don't understand why I have to do all the fanfare and clownery when I can just focus and pull on the moon energy to dump it in the pot." I glowered at said pot although it wasn't its fault. It wasn't mine either but here we were.

"Because that is exactly what we are trying to avoid them seeing." Exhaling a breath that must've come from her toes, she threw herself dramatically with an arm slung over her eyes in the armchair next to the window.

The rapping of knuckles on the door came a second before it opened and River popped his head in, his gaze finding mine immediately like he knew exactly where in the room I would be. Crinkles formed at the corners of his eyes when he saw me with my arms up like a dumbass, although I dropped them to my sides a second too late.

"Can I help?" He gave us puppy eyes as if that would change anything.

"No." We both said adamantly at the same time.

"I mean, I can be quiet and just watch..." He attempted to push the door further open and enter but we both shouted for him to get out, reaching for pillows to throw at his face.

With a chuckle that could curl toes, he ducked out and slammed the door closed.

"And you want me to do that in front of a ritual chamber full of people," I complained again. "Everyone will see me looking like an idiot. I'll never live it down, Sissily. I have an image to maintain."

She rolled her eyes at me.

"What?" Bending down to readjust the stupid flowerpot

Amber gave us to use for the practice, I continued my muttering nonsense. "I do."

"First you need a life to maintain because I dislike Necromancers with a passion, and I don't want to have to deal with one of them in order to bring your ass back if you end up dead." She sounded so reasonable that I almost started nodding my agreement. "Then we can worry about your image."

"I still don't have the urge to do this after your speech."

"You can dress in your favorite designers while doing the spell." No one but your best friend knows how to bribe you. "Put your Louboutins and you'll slay them in many ways, not just unmatched talent. Not that you need fashion now that you have magic."

Reminding me of the times I used to tell her I had to use my impeccable fashion sense because that was the only thing going for me since I had no magic gave me nostalgic feelings for those times. It calmed down the indignant mood I was in, too, and all the fight left my body. Life was much less complicated back then.

"Okay, I'll..." I started but the rapping on the door cut me off.

Sissily and I looked at each other and dove for the throw pillows at the same time. When the door opened, we threw them as hard as we could at River as soon as he poked his head in. But they never hit their mark, instead smacking the wall next to the door and dropping on the floor. Because it wasn't River who entered.

"That's not nice." Jack pouted with his skinny arms crossed over his narrow chest.

"Sorry, buddy." I rushed to hug him. "We thought it was River and we told him not to interfere."

"You're lying, Hazel." He stretched away from me like a

noodle so I didn't pick him up. "It couldn't be River because he is very busy right now."

"Oh really?" Curiosity got the better of me and jealousy that the pigeon was too busy cozying up with some female followed right after. "Busy doing what, exactly?"

"Jack, you don't need to tell her anything." Sissily, knowing me too well, jumped in to prevent a disaster, but the kid ignored her.

"He's busy scaring the human who came looking for you." Jack snickered gleefully. "My dad is there with him, too. The human is brave, but he did look a little pale when mom told me to quickly come find you."

"Oh, my goodness," Sissily let out exactly what I was thinking.

Snatching my shoes, I jumped on each foot while putting them on and ushered Jack and Sissily out of the room. "Lead the way, Jack."

My best friend slid down the wooden floors in her socked feet, not worried about shoes at all. Thankfully no one cared much about decorum around the house, but I grew up with Danika and as I'd like to repeat often, old habits die hard.

"They are in my dad's office." Jack took it as a game and ran ahead of us, his little legs working extra hard to stay a few steps in front. "My mom and Stella are there too. My sister said the human was dreamy." He scrunched up his nose before rushing down the stairway. "But he was awake. Not sleeping. Stella is silly sometimes."

"Yeah, kid, that's what she meant." Sissily snorted, and I elbowed her.

"He's a kid. Don't be a jerk." I muttered but Jack as a shifter didn't miss that.

"I'm not a kid. I'm this tall now." Jumping as he power-walked, he stretched his arm toward the ceiling. "I'm all grown."

"You answer him." I tugged on Sissily's shirt. "I still have a serum in me."

"Oh, so you don't have to answer if you want!" She grinned triumphantly. "Perfect! We can work with that." When I just blinked at her, she looked at Jack. "Of course, you are all grown now Jack. My mistake. It's an old habit."

"It's okay, Sissily." The kid told her with such a serious face the two of us stopped next to him in front of the office without rushing in. "You are allowed to forget sometimes."

I was ready to squish him for being so cute when he continued talking because he wasn't done.

"You're old. It happens." He smiled at her sweetly while she looked like someone fed her rotten fish.

I couldn't help it.

Hecate knows I tried.

Bending over, I laughed so loud and so hard that tears rolled down my cheeks and my stomach hurt. Poor kid stood there for a long while before losing the battle and joining in, his giggles high pitched and addictive.

"It's okay." With a chortle, I wiped my eyes with the sleeve of my shirt and petted Sissily's shoulder before she slapped my hand away. "At your age you're allowed to forget."

"Shut the fuck up, jerk." She shoved me to the side but smiled at Jack who had no idea why she was upset or why I was dying laughing. He just wanted to join in on the fun.

"Language." I gasped and doubled over again.

"At my age, I'm allowed to say whatever the hell I want." She tugged on her shirt to straighten it then grabbed the door and yanked it open without knocking. "Now get out of my way."

I still had tears running down my face, and I was laughing with my mouth open so wide my tonsils were visible from the moon when I locked gazes with the human Jack told us about. Icy blue eyes full of fury zeroed in on mine, and all the humor died in my throat.

It felt like it'd been ten lifetimes since the last time I'd seen the man sitting in Alex's office with River looming over him like a bad omen. But the human didn't look intimidated. If anything, he came across annoyed. Or that could've been because I knew all his tells and quirks so I read him easier. Because River didn't appear aware of the result of his looming presence, he just glowered down his nose.

"Hazel." Davon stood up, unavoidably pushing River slightly back. Intentionally? Probably.

"Davon?" Rushing to wipe my face down and straighten my clothes, I took Jack's hand and walked in. "What in the world are you doing here?"

"Looking for you," he said simply, ignoring everyone else in the room.

"But how did you know to look for me here?"

"Yes, human. How did you know?" River growled low in his throat.

"You forget that I am a police officer." Davon squared his shoulders. "It's my job to find things out."

I just stared at him blankly.

"Your grandmother told me you were here," he admitted.

"Fuck." Sissily hissed.

"Language." Alex and I shouted at the same time, and she slapped a hand over her mouth.

"Danika had a drink," I told no one in particular.
I didn't need to know how to perform a spell.
I needed a miracle.

Chapter Fifteen

"We told him that you've been here the entire time and he needs to leave." River stepped closer to me, effectively blocking my way to Davon.

"Why?" Sticking my head out to look around River, I pinned Davon with my eyes. "Where did you think I was?"

"We had reports coming all day about a woman with your description fighting a guy in the middle of the street in downtown Cleveland." Falling into his cop persona had always been easy for Davon. He pulled out a small black notebook from the back of his pants and opened it up. "Where were you around noon?"

My mouth opened, but Sissily slapped a hand over it so hard, my skin started burning immediately. My ouch as a form of protest was muffled as she held me tight.

"Here," she answered the now frowning Davon. "She was here with me. Helping me…" she looked from Alex to River for help but none came. "Helping me garden. Yes, that's what we were doing. Planting seeds."

"Hazel was gardening?" Davon sounded choked up. "Hazel Byrne was planting seeds?"

Annoyed, I yanked Sissily's hand away from my mouth. "Don't sound so surprised." He looked at me dubiously. "I can plant seeds." There was absolutely no reason for me to sound defensive, yet I did.

"Hazel can do a lot of gardening." Jack jumped in to help and I nearly smiled at him until he finished his sentence. "She makes trees stand up from the ground and they can kill you."

Sissily laughed so loud I cringed from the sound, but she was already on the move, snatching a wiggling Jack in her arms and taking him out the door. "Kids, am I right? Such imagination." Still laughing hysterically like a woman possessed, she slammed the door behind her and the shouting Jack.

"Killing trees?" Davon shook his head and shoved the rolled-up notebook not too gently back in his pocket. "Listen, Hazel, I have no idea what's going on here, but I thought you would rather see me take a statement from you than one of my colleagues."

That's when I noticed the lines tugging down around his mouth, the smudges under his eyes and the sunken cheeks. Davon was still a handsome man, supernaturally so if you remembered he was human, but I could tell that he was tired and hanging at the end of the rope with his patience.

"I rather you do it." I didn't need a truth serum to tell him that.

"Since I last saw you, the city has gone crazy." On a sigh, he brushed a hand over his face. "We have reports of monsters that we can't find, dead bodies are piling up, no one shares any information on your coven being torn apart not once but twice, and now I have over fifty witnesses with the same story that a woman who looks exactly like you made the street split in half and grew a wall of thick roots before making a guy explode."

I swallowed thickly, careful not to say a word.

"The roots are still raised ten feet in the air by the way. I saw them."

I just looked at him.

"If I didn't know you had no magic, I would've brought a van with me and arrested all of you." He ended on a sigh.

"If you know she has no power, why are you here?" Alex folded his hands at the back of his head and stretched in his chair like he had not a care in the world.

"Because I don't know what else to do," Davon told him truthfully.

That was something I always liked in the human. There were no pretenses with Davon. No second guessing or assumptions. He was never too proud to admit when he was wrong or to forgive if you apologized. He didn't hold grudges.

I did.

For a lifetime.

"Tell me you had nothing to do with it." Davon beseeched me with his eyes as much as his words.

"She had nothing to do with it." River's tone was clipped.

"She can speak for herself." The cop puckered his eyebrows as he eyed River up and down. "You are that new guy her grandmother employed in the coven. I remember you."

"I remember you, too." Coming out of Blackman's mouth, it sounded more like a threat.

"This ain't a cock fight," I mumbled and Alex guffawed from behind the desk.

Surprisingly, the Alpha didn't tell Davon to get off his property, nor did he call his betas to escort him home. He was watching the human with a calculating gaze, and I had to wait to see the result of that observation. Whatever it was, I had to make sure Davon left Pack lands in one piece and alive.

"I have a morgue with no more room for new bodies." Leaning forward in his chair, he pressed his forearms on his knees and stared up at the Alpha, unknowing that that position helped him more than anything he could've said. "We get calls with the strangest, outlandish stories we've heard in our lives and most of the time when we go there, there's no trace of their monsters, or them. We find empty, abandoned houses, families and apartments. It's like living in a twilight zone and in the center of it is her coven. They started taking over human cases now too."

My eyebrows dipped low over my eyes hearing that. We never got involved in human cases. We took care of our own and only helped the human law enforcement or military if they requested our involvement.

"I have no problem with you guys helping, don't get me wrong. What I do have a problem with is none of them are solved." A humorless laugh exploded out of Davon. "All cases are closed unsolved. Covered up more like it, and our hands are tied to reopen them. No jurisdiction, we are told."

"I didn't know any of that, Davon. I can promise you I had nothing to do with it." Speaking solely about the cases he mentioned, I did tell him the truth but not about the Anger demon from downtown.

Davon just needed to hear me say something, I guessed, because his shoulders visibly sagged and curved inward from relief. Gratitude softened his features that were unusually tense and he puffed up his cheeks before blowing out a breath.

"Thank you, Hazel." His murmured words blended into one breath. "I just prayed that you had nothing to do with it. Whatever is going on stinks of bad news. I didn't want you to be involved."

If he only knew. Guilt stabbed me that I manipulated the conversation to avoid telling him the truth.

He looked lost.

Something Alex concluded as well because he rose in his chair and leaned on the desk to get closer to the human.

"What can *Me* and *Mine* do to help you, human?" Coming from the Alpha Greywood, that was like whatever god you believed in answering your prayers. By the widening of Davon's eyes, I think he knew it too. "I can hear it in your voice that you care for Hazel."

A low growl started in River's throat that would mistake him for a shifter not a witch-angel hybrid. Maybe he spent too much time around the wolves and he needed to go away. That sounded like a great idea but until then I elbowed him to cut it out.

Alex started at Blackman for a long moment before returning his attention to Davon who had zero self-preservation skills and was nodding affirmatively at the Alpha.

"Just so happens that I, as well as all of mine, care about Hazel and her wellbeing, too. I'm willing to offer whatever assistance you need to keep her safe."

"So, all of this did have something to do with her?" Davon perked up like someone poked him in the butt. He was always a very perceptive guy, unfortunately.

"The less questions you ask, the more assistance you will get." Pinning him with an Alpha stare and adding power behind it, Alex waited a moment before he continued. "Let's say I have young children and I want them to grow up in a safe city. I am willing to help."

Davon looked from me to Alex and back a few times as well as giving River a wary glance. I could see his mind churning behind his blue eyes, but he had always been a practical person. More logic than passion. That was where we as a couple went wrong. I knew he would do what was best for the city and the people he swore to protect.

"I'm willing to take any help you give." He finally turned away from me and fully focused on Alex. "Even if my Captain disagrees, I'll work with you alone as long as the bodies stop piling up."

"Speak with whoever is in charge and let me know." Opening a drawer Alex pulled out a business card and stuck it in Davon's direction. "Call me and I'll come down to the precinct to talk to them if they are willing."

With a sharp nod Davon stood up. "Appreciated." Leaning forward, he reached his arm out and shook Alex's hand with two firm pumps. "I'll be in touch."

My sigh of relief was short lived when the human paused halfway to the door and turned toward me.

"Can I speak with you in private, Hazel?"

River blocked his view of me. I wanted to punch him in the kidney, although I didn't want to speak alone with Davon while I had a truth serum in me.

"Maybe another time?" Walking around Blackman, I ignored his glare. "We have some important things to do. Me and Alex." I waved a hand between me and the Alpha in case he didn't know who we were. "I'll call you."

Suspicion narrowed Davon's gaze immediately. And as I

said, he had no self-preservation sense. He ignored the two dangerous males in the room and walked up to me so close the tips of our shoes were touching. I craned my neck to keep eye contact.

"Are you here of your own free will?" he searched my gaze with his. "No one is forcing you to stay here?"

I blinked my surprise at him.

"Umm, yeah?" it came out as a question because I wasn't expecting it.

"I don't care how scary these guys are, Hazel. If they are holding you against your will, I'll shoot our way out of here if I need to. Tell me the truth, don't be afraid." He took both my hands in his. "I have your back, just say the word."

I didn't deserve the loyalty he continued to show me, but I'd take it. With a smile, I extracted my hands from his so I could throw my arms around his shoulders and give him a hug. He startled at the display of affection at first but sank into my embrace a second later. His arms tightened around my ribcage, and I thought I heard him sniff my hair.

"No one is holding me hostage, Davon I promise." Extracting myself was harder because he reluctantly released me. "These are my friends"—glancing at Alex who was watching everything with little too much interest I amended my words—"they are family. I'm safer here than anywhere else."

He gave me a nod after a while and turned to leave. "The offer still stands. You have my number," he threw over his shoulder and jerked the door open.

Sissily stumbled inside, windmilling her arms so she didn't faceplant on the floor.

"I'll be in touch." Davon ignored her theatrics and walked out, leaving the door open.

"What?" My best friend grunted. "I was ready to rush in and tackle her if she said something dumb."

Covering my face with both hands, I listened to Alex howl with laughter.

River didn't even crack a smile.

Chapter Sixteen

"You'll be fine. Just stay here and I'll get Danika away from the vultures. We can explain everything to her," Sissily murmured while peeking through the crack of a barely open door of the empty office we were hiding in when the delegation arrived.

We'd come full cycle with this whole craziness.

On a good note, this office didn't have a liquor bar. It had no furniture at all.

After Davon left, Alex told us to get ready because we were going to the Coven building. He organized a whole convoy of shifters to come with us, not leaving it to chance when it came to our safety. With wolves being implicated in a couple of situations which put his family and pack in danger, the Alpha was ready for heads to roll.

So was I for that matter.

Guards were posted all around the Gatekeeper's coven, ready to intervene at a moment's notice. We just needed to get my grandmother away from the delegation who was circling her like the vultures Sissily accused them of being.

"I know I'll be fine." Pressing my hand on the door, I closed it almost on her nose. "What I don't know is why we are sneaking around. We can just go join them, and I'll drag Danika away from them."

"We will alert them that something is up," my friend insisted, pushing me away and peeking through the barely opened door again. "When they see all of us together, the jig is up, woman. Haven't you watched any movies? When all the main agents gather together to confront someone, everyone knows it's over for the bad guys."

"This is not a movie," I drawled, unimpressed by her metaphor.

"Just trust me." She smoothed her clothing and gave me a pointed look. "I'll go get her. If I'm not back in five minutes, something is wrong."

"You are insane." I told her, but she was already closing the door behind her. With a sigh, I turned to the two males leaning on the wall on the other side of the empty office. "She's insane," I repeated as if they hadn't heard me the first time.

"We don't want to alert them to our presence yet," Alex agreed with Sissily's idea. "Well, my presence, I should say. Or Blackman's. The more we have them on their toes the easier they'll give themselves away."

"If you say so." I shrugged.

I just wanted this over and done with.

Also, I was annoyed that River hadn't said a word to me since Davon left. He had no right to be upset because I neither invited the human nor did I know he was coming. And it wasn't like something was going on between us and he had a right to be jealous. It wasn't me sleeping around the Greywood pack, either.

The door opened to save me from my internal torment

and Sissily rushed inside before Danika joined her. My grandmother, as always, brought the air of self-importance with her that she wore like a cloak. It made everyone around her hunch their shoulders under the weight of it. None of us did, however, so she dropped all pretenses as soon as the door was closed behind her.

"What is the meaning of this?" Her cold stare moved over each of us like an accusing finger. "Care to explain, Miss Stormblood?"

I searched her face for the scar I'd left not even twelve hours ago but I only found smooth unmarred skin.

"We came across new information that you should know." Alex pushed away from the wall and started telling my grandmother everything we found out from the witch I intercepted in the building to Davon coming to Pack land and sharing the problems the human law enforcement had around the city.

She listened intently, not blinking, and her chest barely moved with her breaths. The longer she was silent the faster my heart was beating. When someone tried to cross her, she would be unnaturally still, but I could always feel her anger like a living thing lashing at everyone around. As she stood there the same way she always did with her spine ram-rod straight and head held high, I could feel...

Nothing.

I didn't feel anything at all, which creeped me the hell out.

"You must've ingested some of the alcohol, as well," Alex was saying while I was internally freaking out because I refused to acknowledge what was in front of me. "I figured as much when the human said you told him where Hazel was."

Danika's dead stare locked on my face, and I knew in that moment she was aware that I saw everything clearly. The air thickened with the stench of ozone the same second River materialized next to me, his shoulder bumping mine. The pigeon could sense the threat, as well.

"They poured potions in my drinks?" Danika spoke slowly, not taking her eyes off me.

"Truth serum as far as we know," Sissily shared dutifully, standing straighter in Danika's presence out of respect for her station.

"And Hazel took it." It was not a question.

"Yes," I heard my best friend say while internally I was screaming no.

"We told everything we know. We should leave now," I addressed Alex without looking at him and saw from the corner of my eye that he'd picked up on my unease. "So they don't notice something's up," I added as an afterthought.

Sissily frowned at my behavior, but she knew me too well not to pick up on how freaked out I was. She inched away from Danika and moved toward me as subtly as she could.

"You are here already." My grandmother never took her eyes off me. "We should go to the ritual chamber so you can perform the spell. With that out of the way, we can focus on the rest of the mess on our doorstep."

"I haven't practiced enough." It wasn't a lie. "I should do it a few more times before the full delegation sees me mess up."

"Magic is who we are, Hazel." She dismissed me as always. "Don't be dramatic. It's as easy as breathing. Just follow the spell."

Seeing as there was no way out of here without fighting Danika, which I was not prepared to do, I gave her a clipped nod so I could buy myself time to think. Away from my grandmother where I could take a breath with full lung capacity. Talk to my friends, too, and prepare a plan of action where all of us were on the same page.

Danika had caught us off guard as always.

"Before I leave"—she was almost to the door, gliding toward it like the snake she was, but she turned—"can you siphon magic from a person, Hazel?"

All the blood in my veins curdled at that question.

"I have no idea what my magic could do." It wasn't a lie, but I answered too quickly. I screwed up, and I knew it.

The Alpha's face darkened at her question.

A small smile played on Danika's lips as she opened the door and exited the empty office with a flare of a phoenix rising from the ashes.

Bitch.

"She knew," I let out and sagged as soon as Sissily grabbed my elbow. My knees couldn't hold me.

"She would never..." my best friend started but trailed off when she took a look at my face. I bet there was no blood left in it.

"She knew about the potion, about the dead bodies, about everything." My lips were numb; I could barely feel them move.

"To what end?" Alex started pacing like a caged lion. "You are her blood. This is insanity."

"I doubt she wants me dead. For now."

"You mean this whole thing is part of whatever plan she has?" Sissily's nails were digging into my skin but I doubt she was aware of it. Slowly, she lowered us to the floor. I guessed her knees got wobbly too. "Delores earlier today, the Anger demon, all of it?"

"I don't remember who is present in the delegation that she would want gone apart from Delores," River mused above us. "And how is she planning to force you to steal someone's magic even if you could? That witch would be erased from existence if you are capable of something like that. We are nothing without the magic."

"I need to get out of here." Pushing myself up and taking Sissily with me, I darted toward the door.

Alex and River were right behind us, wordlessly agreeing that it was a great plan. That was until I yanked the door open and came face to face with the male witch who'd been accompanying my grandmother everywhere. His grin was wide and genuine, but the sparkle in his eye was missing.

"Miss Byrne, such a pleasure again." He purred so perfectly I could've mistaken him for a shifter and not a witch.

"I'm busy, excuse me." I tried to move around him, but he blocked my way.

Alex growled deep in his chest.

"Move out of my way." I sounded feral too when I spoke.

"I'm afraid I can't do that, Miss Byrne. You are expected in the main ritual chamber." He did sound apologetic, I had to give him that.

"And if I don't go?" Jutting my chin out, I dared him to say something stupid so I could turn him into an anthill.

The witch looked down the hallway and his gaze turned sad. With a dread pulling in the pit of my stomach and a ball forming in my throat the size of a fist, I leaned out to see what he was looking at.

My heart dropped to the floor and splattered at my feet when I found a blue widened gaze staring back at me. Davon had his hands tied behind his back and tape was stuck across his mouth. Two young witches, I hadn't seen them before, held him by the arms while he struggled to free himself.

Sissily gasped behind me.

"Lead the way." I told the delegation member. "What was your name? Sorry I never asked."

"Viktor," River spat as he followed the rest of us. "Victor Ocean. High priest of Greece."

"Always a pleasure Blackman." Victor sent a crooked smile at River.

"I should've known Danika never plays fair." Not caring if Victor heard me I continued to blabber incoherent things.

"She just thought you needed a little encouragement to add passion into your performance." The asshole thought my muttering was an invitation for a chat. "Surely you can't be that attached to the human." He looked pointedly at River when he said that.

I fumed.

If anger could be visible, I would've been a ball of inferno.

Too soon, we entered the ritual chamber, and I was ushered to the altar while my friends were stopped near the doors, two witches guarding each of them.

Grateful that they trusted me enough to not start fighting yet, I looked around the room, watching the full delegation clustered at the center with Danika at the front. Not even a flicker of emotion was on her face.

"Who are you?" I mouthed, my face twisted with disgust. She'd always been a bitch and power hog but this was beyond anything I ever expected. She'd sunk so low nothing could get her out of it.

"You can begin." A female that used to hang out with Sasha the bully sneered at me from my right.

"Come lie down on the altar and I will." I sneered back, making her take a step back before she caught herself.

"Enough." Danika amplified her voice, and I jumped when it boomed in the closed room. "Begin, Hazel."

Swallowing everything I wanted to say, I closed my eyes and counted to ten. I could do this. I might look like a fool and butch up some of the words but I'd give it a valiant effort. Because if I did the spell, she had no other reason to keep us here. Or Davon.

Poor Davon, I had to get him out of here.

Ignoring everyone and their insistent muttering, I focused on lighting the four candles that were already placed on each corner of the altar. As the flames started dancing around, I picked up a Palo Santo stick with a charred tip and lit it to clear the space. As soon as the smoke curled around me, a calm fell over my shoulders that helped me stay centered.

Humming to myself, I walked around the altar, waving the smoke and cleansing the air so it was a pure space where magic could bloom. Thinking of all the times I wished I could do this, I wanted to puke. Putting down the stick in a small dish of sand, I picked up a selenite tower and placed it at the center of the altar. Moving the small flowerpot—which Sissily must've brought in the chamber when she went to fetch Danika—I filled it with fresh soil from a round dish I found near the base of the altar.

A commotion made me look up to find my best friend arguing with the two witches that were guarding her, and after a moment, they let her dart to where I was standing.

"I told them I had to give you the seed," she muttered under her breath and dug an actual seed from her pocket.

"What is it?" I asked, just to say something because I wanted to scream and run otherwise.

"I have no idea." She gripped my fingers so tight I felt my bones crack. Her fingers were ice cold. "You can do this."

"I can do this," I repeated, and they ripped her away from me.

Anger churned inside me.

All the whispers stopped when I cleared my throat. Adjusting the pot until I was happy where it was, I blew a breath over it and the soil before doing the same to the seed. Gently, I placed it inside and drew a pentagram in the air above it. Raising both arms, fingers stretching as high as they could go, I took a breath and chanted what Sissily taught me.

"Mother Goddess lend me your light,
Give me your power on this faithful night,
I invoke you into my being and soul,
Fill up my vessel and make me feel whole,
I stand before you in awe and in love,
I cherish the gifts you send from above,
I ask you tonight to show unto me,
My mother, My Goddess, so mote it be."

Strong winds started circling around the altar whipping my hair around my face. I continued to chant the same thing over and over while pushing my magic down every time it wanted to lash out. Bright light blinded me, and I lowered my hands to hold them over the flowerpot a long minute. When the light was gone, I slowly opened my eyes. A red dahlia was between my palms sticking out a good ten inches above the soil.

Applause exploded in the chamber, startling the crap out of me, and I blinked up at all the grinning faces. They thought this was a circus and I was a monkey. Anger coiled inside me, but I pushed it down. I did what Danika wanted; I was taking Davon and my friends and we were getting out of here.

I moved to leave, but I was cut mid step.

"Not so fast." Danika glided toward me while the rest of them still chirped and oohed over how wonderful the spell was. "Bring her," she told someone I couldn't see.

My heart stopped when they dragged Delores in the chamber and dropped her at my feet. The witch was dazed, and her hair was matted. There was no blood on her, thank the goddess.

"Siphon her magic," Danika hissed at me. "There is a punishment for betraying your kind," she announced to the group. "Debt must be paid."

"You are out of your mind," I told her, already turning away from both of them.

I came here to cover my ass up not give my freaky nature away.

A gasp was stolen from my lips when my grandmother snatched me by the arm, lifting me to my toes and got in my face.

"I need her essence to trade it for my soul. I said siphon her magic now, Hazel."

Dread spread like a wave through my body, and I felt numb. She didn't care about me or anyone else. All Danika wanted was to clear out her mess. It mattered nothing to her that when the witches saw me do something like that they would stop at nothing to destroy me. She wanted something. No matter the price.

My eyes found Davon who was as pale as a sheet in one corner of the room.

Something inside me flipped. I no longer cared who knew I was a freak. Or what I could do. The rest of them wanted me dead already. Obviously, Danika did too.

A smile stretched my lips, and Danika frowned at me.

Oppressive silence spread around the room.

"Alex?" I called out to my friend.

"I'm here, Hazel." There was no hesitation in his tone. Tears pricked my eyes.

"Please take Davon out of here," I asked him.

"What's the meaning of this?" Danika snapped when the Alpha half shifted and shouldered his way toward the human. "Mr. Greywood, stop this instant."

"I don't answer to you, Danika," he snarled and ripped Davon away from the witches, tossing him over his shoulder.

I unleashed the magic who was eagerly waiting for this very moment. Screams split the air when all of them were lifted off the ground and slammed like flies on the walls of the chamber. I left Danika for last. It was comical to see her eyes widen when I picked her up with a rope of my magic and slapped her next to the rest on the wall. Her head lolled to the side, but I didn't care. Holding them where they were took effort, but I rushed to where Sissily and River stood so they could help guide me while I held everyone in place.

"What's the plan?" My best friend added her own magic to help me zap everyone still awake with lightning.

"I'm not a killer like her, let's go." Gratefully taking River's offered hand, I let him guide me out so I could maintain the power.

"She's going to come after us now." Sissily gasped when

we ran down the hallway, listening to the shrieks as the witches came to.

"I'm hoping for that," I told her.

"Really?" River sounded intrigued.

"Oh yeah, Blackman." Grinning from ear to ear, I followed Alex out the double doors. "Danika is about to find out that payback is a bitch!"

Also By Maya Daniels

vinci-books.com/devildetails

Heaven wants me dead, Hell wants me on a leash. I just want out.

Hi, I'm Helena and I accidentally opened a portal to Hell. Now, I'm dodging angels, making deals with demons, and trying not to fall for the ridiculously handsome one who claims we're "destined." Spoiler: I'm definitely not buying it. Either way, I'm screwed.

Turn the page for a free preview…

The Devil is in the Details: Chapter One

HELENA

One week ago

The city passes in a blur as I stare out the window, unseeing, while I replay the last few hours yet again. *'What if's'* have never been my favorite to start with, but I can't help thinking that if we'd done anything differently, then maybe, just maybe, I wouldn't have this gnawing feeling that my life took a nosedive off a cliff and it's headed straight for the jutting rocks at the bottom. *What did I miss?* Questions rattle in my brain, causing my temples to pound with their own heartbeat.

"This should be our last stop before we head back."

George yanks me out of my thoughts when his deep, rusty voice echoes in my ears. I hate the earpieces they make us wear, even though I know how useful they are. Well, useful for the rest of them, anyway; I'm more than capable of taking care of myself. There's no reason for him to use it because we're all sitting in his car, but he likes being a jerk. Glaring at the back of his head, I fight the urge to smack his head on the steering wheel he's clutching in his paw-sized hands like the thing is trying to escape. If you call him out on it, you'll have to listen to lectures of how he makes sure the equipment is working, so the rest of us just grind our teeth and say nothing. There's five of us in the car. Jared, Cass, and Amanda act like it doesn't bother them, but I see their jaws ticking in the occasional light we pass.

Lost in my thoughts, I was enjoying the quiet after our last stop, especially since one of the abominations managed to draw blood before I sent him where he belongs. We are the chosen hunters in North America that protect humans from all things that go bump in the night. Entrusted and blessed by the Archangels themselves—or so we are told—we mostly hunt demons, with an occasional vamp or shifter mixed in. The last stop was a suburb of Atlanta, Georgia, where three demons had nested and had terrorized humans for over a month. Possessing them, they jumped from one body to the next and turned a lovely quiet neighborhood into something from nightmares. Out of nowhere, domestic violence blossomed, neighbors killed each other, and fires and break-ins happened every night. It put a red dot on the area, and we were dispatched to investigate. Needless to say, the demons are no more, and I'll pray that the neighborhood goes back to the idyllic picture the lawns and homes suggested it used to be.

Lifting my arm towards the window, I check to see if the scratch one of the demons left by raking its claws on me has healed. Only thin pink lines are still visible, but those will be gone by the time I take a shower and wash the grime and blood off me. There will be nothing left, not even a scar, but I'll remember the demon's words clearly: *Soon all of you will regret getting involved in things that you know nothing about.* Its raspy voice rattles through my brain.

All of us are blessed with fast healing, longer lifespans, speed, and strength. I would like to think I'm still human, but with each new day after my eighteenth birthday three years ago, I doubt that statement more and more. To make matters worse, I'm even different from the rest of them. My sixth sense is like a GPS for evil, even when the others can't see demons or any of the other evil creatures that plague humanity. It's almost as if evil calls to me, daring me to find it. One thing I've never told anyone is that when that feeling starts inside my chest, it's like I'm about to receive the greatest gift of my life. Excitement and giddiness course through my veins, making me sick to my stomach. It should feel repulsive, yet it doesn't. I've lied to everyone I call friends and family, telling them that it's a sickening feeling because I don't want anyone doubting my loyalties. My conscience is not clear.

"It should be around the corner," George speaks through the earpiece again, making me physically flinch. Instinctively my fist lifts, going straight for the back of his head. Unnerved by the entire night, I'm barely able to control the anger still coursing through me, and he's pushing it. I know, because his dark eyes lock with mine in the rearview mirror every time he does it.

Fast as lightning, Amanda grabs my forearm, and her bright pink nails dig into my flesh. "That's good! We can get it done and go home," she says, emphasizing *home* like she's not glaring at me in the back seat.

Amanda's pink pixie cut hair is styled in teal-tipped spikes on top of her head. Large brown eyes shaded with glittery eyeshadow and sparkly mascara on the long lashes blink from her porcelain face. She looks almost like a doll.

Like those anime characters that she loves so much. We've been best friends ever since I can remember, and no one knows me as well as she does. No wonder she snatched my arm before my fist connected with the back of George's head.

"Yes, I'm actually looking forward to the 'go home' part!" Cass snickers, smacking Jared on the shoulder, making his body twist in the passenger seat to look at her over his shoulder. His blue eyes light up, and he gives her a beaming smile when she grins at him.

"Oh boy! I'm gonna be sick." Amanda groans, rolling her eyes dramatically. "The lovey-dovey googly eyes make me sick." She turns to me again, pretending to gag. My arm slowly lowers, and she stops digging her nails into my flesh, petting my forearm gently before releasing it.

"Yeah." Taking a deep breath, I lean back in my seat and turn to look out the window. "Go in, get out, go home, and no lovey-dovey googly eyes. It works for me."

"Of course, it works for you, Hel! You wouldn't know what googly eyes were if they hit you in the face." Amanda giggles, smacking my thigh with the back of her hand. "Ouch! Move those guns, would you?" She glares at my weapons as if it's their fault she hit her hand on them.

"Leave the girls alone! They're fine just where they are." Petting them affectionately, I glare back at her.

The SUV makes a left turn, and we forget all about the conversation. All the streetlights are broken, and the street is pitch black. Our headlights light up a quarter of it. Bodies with missing parts are haphazardly tossed around like a zombie Apocalypse movie set. My stomach clenches and my entire body coils up, ready to fight as energy rushes through me. Tension rises inside the car as the three of us lean forward from the back seat to see better. This is not something we see every day, even in our line of work. The abominations are getting bolder by the minute, but at least it can't get worse than this.

George flicks on his high beams, and we take a sharp collective intake of breath at the gruesome view revealed in front of us. I was wrong. Crouched above piles of dozens of dead humans are gray, wrinkled demons, their arrow-pointed tails flicking like cats' while they tear the flesh off the bones they clutch in claw-tipped hands. Their heads snap in our direction, revealing red glowing eyes and gaping mouths full of razor-sharp shark teeth. Looking like aliens, with only eyes and a mouth, blood drips down their grotesque faces as they hiss in unison. Everyone else in the car froze, but the anger that I've been fighting all night bubbles like a volcano in my chest. I push the door open and jump out of the car.

"Hel, no!" Amanda's scream pierces the night, but I slam the door in her face.

Pulling both of my revolvers out of their holsters, the usual calm engulfs me like a blanket. Feeling their comforting weight in my hands, I smile at the hissing abominations that turn towards me.

"Playtime, motherfuckers!"

All the abominations spring into action with an eerie screech. Like mice trying to escape a flood, a horde of them bound in my direction. The high beams of the car at my back make it easier to pick them off one by one. The sound of the gunshots energizes me with its beauty. The demons dropped one by one like rocks, their bodies causing those behind to trip and roll on the cracked, uneven concrete of the street.

Shadows move at the corner of my eye as the rest of my team joins me. Blades, throwing stars, and knives fly in the air as they take down more demons. Shouts and hoots sound above my shots as we add more bodies to this street of nightmares, where so many unfortunate innocent humans lost their lives tonight. The pink scars on my forearm throb for no reason, making me hesitate long enough to realize the demons are not trying to fight or defend themselves. They are dying in their attempts to get to me. My team spreads around me like a circle, guarding my back while I'm in shock at the horrifying thought. I almost drop my guns, which makes rage bubble up in my chest. None of them will escape tonight.

That night, the haunting screeching didn't stop until the early hours. It's a night the five of us will remember for as long as we live. I just pray that my team forgets that none of the abominations tried to kill me. Instead, they died trying to capture me alive. Too bad for them. I'm not easy prey.

The Devil is in the Details: Chapter Two

HELENA

Present Day

Scalding hot water pounds my shoulders as I lean my forearms on the tiles and try to wake up properly. The past week has been one intense hunt after another, and they keep getting more difficult. Even with the fast healing, my entire body hurts; the muscles knotted in my back and shoulders feel like tennis balls under my skin.

We've lost so many hunters that it's morbid to walk through the halls of our home thinking, *Say something, it might be the last time you see them.* No one in the sanctuary talks about what is going on, but we all feel the tension building like a ticking bomb with the patrons. The entire Forbearer's ministry has been holed up in the library, only coming out to send us on hunts in groups. The excitement of the chase has gone. No more jokes or slaps on the back while making plans to hang out when we get back. Now, only dull eyes track our movements, like we are going in front of a firing squad. For many, that is precisely the case.

Lifting my face towards the showerhead, I hope the water can wash away the gloomy thoughts clouding my mind. I have the urge to go kick the doors in, storm the library, and demand answers, but after that cursed night, I have secrets to keep. Secrets that might create a bright flashing arrow pointing at my head with the sign 'Imposter' and a reason for me to defend my loyalties. Goosebumps cover my entire body and a cold wave of nausea hits at that thought. My team is the only one not to lose a hunter, and it's not because we're better than the rest. The abominations are more interested in getting to me than trying to stay alive. The four people in my group all keep their mouths closed, even though they watch me from the corners of their eyes. There is a new wariness surrounding us.

Loud pounding on the door sounds over the noise of the water. I turn the shower off, smoothing my hands over my face and hair. The liquid glides down my back, but it's painful instead of soothing. Pulling the screen door open and snatching a towel, I hurry to open the door before whoever it is wakes the entire place up.

"There you are!" Amanda prances inside, pushing past me and acting like she didn't just try to break the door in.

"Are we under attack?" Closing the door, I lean back on it, crossing my hands over my chest.

"No." Grinning, she jumps on my bed, bouncing few times before she settles. Innocently, she blinks her big eyes at me.

"Why are you here at 4 AM?" I'm glaring because this is my time, a time when I can think, collect my thoughts, and not worry about anything or anyone.

"I've been waiting for you to let me know when you're ready to talk because I figured you needed time to process what happened." The mask of playfulness is gone. "Since you want to play stupid, I figured I'd invite myself in for a heart to heart talk."

"I have nothing to talk about!" Snapping at her, I gather my clothes, snatching them as if it's their fault I'm grumpy, and walk towards the bathroom to dress.

"I beg to differ, and I assure you that neither you nor I are going out that door until we talk." Her voice floats to the bathroom where I drop everything on the floor and lean on the sink with my head hanging down.

She has a point. I know it. She knows it, too. The problem is that I honestly don't know what to tell her. When I look back on that night a week ago, I hope if I ignore it, it will go away." But I must face the music and get to the bottom of it, no matter what it is.

"Did you hear what the abomination that raked my arm said?" My voice is low, but I don't need to lift my head to know that Amanda is standing at the door. Her eyes poke at my back like accusing fingers.

"No," she says softly, as if scared to speak louder in case I stop talking.

"'Soon, all of you will regret getting involved in things that you know nothing about.'" Lifting my head, I lock eyes with her in the mirror. "After that, we lost dozens every night, and each night only our team comes back with the same number as when we left. They don't fight or even try to protect themselves. They're too busy trying to get their hands on me. You can't tell me that you haven't noticed."

"Oh, I've noticed!" She nods adamantly. "But you're a hot piece of ass, so you can't blame them for wanting all those yummy curves!" Her eyebrows go as high as her hairline and the ring she has on the side of her left eyebrow sparkles in the light. She sighs and stops the charade when I just glare at her. "Listen, girl, they're demons! Who knows why they say and do half the things that they do? Our job is not to exchange pleasantries with them. We're there to kill the suckers and send them back to hell. It's what we've been born to do!" Spreading her hands wide, she looks at me as if expecting applause for the speech.

"What if it was right?" Searching her eyes through the mirror, her forehead furrows. Turning around, I lean on the sink. "What if something has changed that we don't know about? I mean, they've never spoken to us." Frowning, I nibble on my lower lip. "Right? They've never spoken before now?"

"Not that I know of, no." Pursing her lips, it looks painful to admit that fact.

"So, my point is," I say, pointing a finger at her, "Why now? And why me?"

"It could've spoken to anyone if it was a Chatty Cathy." Cocking her head, she looks like she is seriously considering her ridiculous statement.

"Amanda, be serious for a second, please. I'm not joking!"

"I know you're not, Hel." Coming closer, she grabs both my hands in hers, squeezing gently. "You are overthinking, as usual. We're the good guys, remember? There's nothing to question or even think twice about." There is so much sincerity in her big eyes that my chest hurts with how much I want to believe everything she says. If only that damn night hadn't happened. "They tell us where the abominations are, we go send them back to hell, and everyone is happy and safe. The good guys always win."

"The good will always win," I repeat, and the pressure in my head and chest lessens. "Thank you! I think it's just the number of deaths this last week that's messing with my head. It all just hit out of nowhere." Pulling my hands out of hers, I rub them over my face.

"Yeah, I figured it was something like that. You're always the one that takes our losses the hardest. It's not your job to babysit all of us, and you can't save everyone, my fearless, beautiful friend. I just wish you knew what a great person you are and how much we love you for it." Tugging me to her, she wraps her arms around me, squeezing me tight. "Even George, the jerk!" Snickering, she pulls back to look at my glaring face, "I think being a jerk is his way of flirting with you."

I push her away as she laughs in my face while making kissing sounds. Shaking my head, I can't help but laugh with her as I try to place a hand over her mouth to make her stop.

"You're the jerk now! Stop this crap!" Laughing, we wrestle around, and she chortles even louder when I almost lose the towel. The pounding on the door has us both sobering up in a second as I rush to open it, clutching the towel to my chest. George stands at the door and looks me up and down slowly before his dark eyes settle on mine.

"We've been summoned to the library. Another team never made it back." His words feel like punches to my chest as I numbly stare at him.

Grab your copy...
vinci-books.com/devildetails

About the Author

Maya Daniels, USA Today Bestselling and multi-award-winning supernatural suspense author, is a fun-loving woman with many talents.

She traveled the world, gaining life experiences that helped her career as an investigative journalist, as well as her storytelling. Maya writes compelling tales of magic, mythical creatures, loyalty, and life-changing friendships with snarky female characters—much like herself.

Her travels have taken her to Europe, Africa, Asia, Australia, and America. Born with her feet in motion, she currently resides in Ohio, spinning her next epic story that you will not want to put down.

Her biggest 'sins' are her love of chocolate and coffee—through an IV drip! One to never sit still, Maya practices Reiki healing, different types of martial arts, reads about the arcane, talks to furry creatures more than humans, picks up a sledgehammer for home improvement, and travels with her fated mate, seeking her own adventures.

www.ingramcontent.com/pod-product-compliance
Ingram Content Group UK Ltd.
Pitfield, Milton Keynes, MK11 3LW, UK
UKHW040035130426
469799UK00003B/115